EVERYDAY HERO

EVERYDAY HERO

Kathleen Cherry

ORCA BOOK PUBLISHERS

Library and Archives Canada Cataloguing in Publication

Cherry Kathleen, 1964–, author
Everyday hero / Kathleen Cherry.

Issued in print and electronic formats.
ISBN 978-1-4598-0982-6 (pbk.).—ISBN 978-1-4598-0983-3 (pdf).—
ISBN 978-1-4598-0984-0 (epub)

I. Title.
PS8605.H4648E94 2016 jc813'.6 C2015-904500-2
C2015-904501-0

First published in the United States, 2016
Library of Congress Control Number: 2015946189

Summary: When a new friend challenges Alice, who has Asperger Syndrome, to step outside her comfort zone, Alice decides to revise her rules in this novel for middle readers.

Orca Book Publishers is dedicated to preserving the environment and has printed this book on Forest Stewardship Council® certified paper.

Orca Book Publishers gratefully acknowledges the support for its publishing programs provided by the following agencies: the Government of Canada through the Canada Book Fund and the Canada Council for the Arts, and the Province of British Columbia through the BC Arts Council and the Book Publishing Tax Credit.

Cover design by Rachel Page
Cover photo by EyeEm
Author photo by Propel the Mood Photography

ORCA BOOK PUBLISHERS
www.orcabook.com

Printed and bound in Canada.

19 18 17 16 • 4 3 2 1

To every child who has ever felt different.
Individual differences are what make people special
and provide us with unique strengths.

One

If my mother hadn't decided to be a sandwich, I would not have had nine detentions in January.

If I hadn't had nine detentions in January, I would not have met Megan.

If I hadn't met Megan, I would not have been a hero.

To be accurate, my father said that my mother was part of the "sandwich generation." A *generation* means *all the people born and living for a period of approximately thirty years*. A *sandwich* means *two slices of bread with a filling (such as meat, fish, cheese, peanut butter) between them.*

I like to define words. I once tried to memorize all the definitions in *Webster's New World Dictionary*. I stopped at *mineralize*.

I asked Dad what this meant. About Mom being a sandwich, not mineralize. He said it meant that she had to look after her child, me, as well as my grandparents. She is the filling, we are the bread. Truthfully, I am not really a child, being thirteen years, four months and seventeen days old at the time of writing.

Today is April 23.

There is something else you need to know about me. I have Asperger Syndrome, so looking after me is harder than looking after the typical teenager. Asperger Syndrome is on the autism spectrum, but people who have it usually function better than most autistic individuals.

Dad and I arrived in Kitimat on January 2 at 7:37 PM. We moved from Vancouver because Dad got a job. Mom stayed in Vancouver to help my grandparents. My grandma had had a stroke, which Dad said was bad timing.

I started school in Kitimat on January 4.

I got my first detention on January 6 when I sat on the stairs at the north end of the school.

I like stairs. Sitting on the stairs is not against the rules.

Except I was supposed to be in gym class.

This was my first detention. There were only three of us in room 131: Ms. Lawrence, Megan and me. Megan wore black and sat at the back of the class in the second desk from the window.

(I knew she was called Megan because Ms. Lawrence looked at her and said, "Here again, Megan?" Then she sighed with a big wheezing *whoosh*.)

After that, no one said anything.

I didn't say anything. Megan didn't say anything. Ms. Lawrence didn't say anything. I wished I could go to detention instead of school.

***

Usually I achieve good grades in school. I love math and science, and I like English and social studies. I write well. My special-education teacher said that people with Asperger Syndrome can be authors. Some people say that James Joyce, Lewis Carroll and George Orwell were autistic.

I am less competent at speaking though. Thousands of words flood my brain like slippery minnows (this is a simile), and I can't find the right words in the right order.

This means I'm usually silent in class.

Dad once told me that students with Asperger's are often perfect students. I think this might be true except for the head banging. Plus I used to circle the flagpole at my old school. And I like to sit in corners with the walls pressing against me.

By the way, having Asperger Syndrome does not mean I can calculate sums, like 431 divided by 92 and multiplied by 5, which is 23.423913043478260869565217391304. (I only know this because I used a calculator.) People who can do that are sometimes called savants. I am not a savant.

On January 8, I got my second detention. I left the change room before gym even started. I left because the change room stank—of wet socks, sweat, antiperspirant, hair gel, hair spray, perfume, hand sanitizer, hand lotion, sunscreen and Febreze.

I don't like smells. They make me want to wriggle out of my skin. Or bang my head. Or curl up in a corner.

So I left. At my elementary school, this was not against the rules, but middle school is different.

Still, I like detention better than the change room, so I was not upset when I walked into room 131 again.

Ms. Lawrence sat at her desk. She wore a sweatshirt patterned with flowers.

"Another detention?" she said.

Before I could answer, I heard the heavy, rhythmic *clunk...clunk...clunk* of footsteps approaching.

"Not again," Ms. Lawrence muttered, looking toward the door.

Megan was tall. She wore black high-heeled boots, a jean jacket, a black T-shirt with a silver skull on it, and metal chains slung around her neck, waist and wrists. Her long black hair was streaked with purple. She had a silver ring through her bottom lip.

When she entered, everything in the room seemed smaller.

Ms. Lawrence pushed her hand through her short gray hair. "How long do you have to stay this time, Megan?"

"Dunno. Beils sent me."

"You're not on his list. He must have forgotten. I will go and ask *Mr*. Beils." Ms. Lawrence emphasized the word *Mister*. Then she stood and hurried out of the classroom.

"Whatever." Megan shrugged, and the chains jangled as she walked down the aisle of desks toward me.

I am very observant. Sometimes that is a problem. There are so many things to notice—colors, noises, smells, sounds...

And I can't focus on only one thing and ignore another. I cannot notice the skeleton drawn in red ballpoint on the left sleeve of her jean jacket without seeing also the purple bruise under her left eye, the rip in her shirt and the four silver rings on her left hand. I couldn't see her right hand.

"What are you looking at?" Megan asked, running the words together so they sounded like *whatchalookingat*.

"You," I said.

Another thing I should tell you: I can't lie. It's not that I don't want to lie. I'm just no good at it.

"I don't want any punk kid looking at me." Megan leaned over my desk.

This made sense. I don't like people looking at me either.

"And this is *my* place," she added, putting her face close to mine.

Her breath didn't smell.

I looked at the desktop. At my school last year, we wrote our names on laminated yellow cards and placed them on the left-hand corner of our desks.

I couldn't see any laminated yellow cards in room 131.

"What are you doing?" Megan asked, the words again strung together.

"Looking for your name on a laminated yellow card."

"You trying to be funny?" She leaned closer to me, her fingers gripping the desktop. Her nail polish was black and chipped.

"No," I said, because that is another thing about me: I don't understand jokes, so I never try to be funny.

"You looking for a fight?"

"No," I said again.

Megan's hands balled into fists. Now that I could see her right hand, I noticed that she had a thumb ring shaped like a skull.

I looked up to see if I could identify her expression. But I am not good at understanding faces, even though my teacher last year gave me a special feelings chart.

"Just keep out of my face!" Megan turned and walked out of the room with heavy, clunking footsteps, not even waiting for Ms. Lawrence to come back.

So I counted dictionaries in the bookcase—fifteen. I like the number three and multiples of three. I like counting. I'd counted the dictionaries three times before Ms. Lawrence finally came back.

"You're still here?" Her eyebrows rose, disappearing under her bangs.

I nodded.

"Sorry, there was a problem I had to deal with in the girls' washroom. Anyhow, you can go now, um"—she looked at her paper—"Alice."

I stood, swinging my backpack onto my shoulders. It thumped against my spine. I walked into the hall, which was quiet, the dimness broken only by bright rectangles of light at the front entrance.

I went to the outside door and exited into the heavy, damp grayness of a north-coast afternoon. The streetlights shone into the parking lot, and two red taillights disappeared around the corner and onto the main road.

At first I didn't recognize their importance. I did not question why the yard was empty. Or realize that the dimness spoke of late, late afternoon.

And then...

Sweat prickled under my arms. My throat tightened. My breath quickened. I tasted vomit in the back of my throat. I hate vomit—its smell, its taste, its texture.

I rocked on my heels. "One...two...three," I muttered. Counting usually calms me.

"OMG. Are you, like, talking to yourself?"

Megan was leaning against the wall of the school, chewing gum.

I didn't answer because I do not like questions.

"Are you, like, deaf as well?"

I shook my head.

"So can you hear? Can you, like, talk too?"

I counted the cars still parked in the teachers' parking lot—nine. Good.

"When did you get here?" Megan asked.

I looked at my watch. "Four minutes ago."

She laughed. "OMG. You are, like, seriously wacked."

I counted the cars again. Nine is a good number because it is divisible by three.

I counted the nine cars nine times. Nine times nine is eighty-one.

Another bus arrived. I squinted in the bright light of its headlights. It stopped with a whine of brakes. The door opened. The yellow glare of its interior lights flooded outward. The sign above the windshield read *City Center*.

That's how I knew it wasn't my bus. I take the After-School Special, and the sign above the windshield always reads *After-School Special*.

Megan pushed past me, stepping onto the bus, her chains rattling.

The bus driver leaned forward in his chair. "Coming?"

I am not supposed to talk to strangers. It is a rule. I like rules.

"What bus do you want?" he asked.

I did not say anything because he was a stranger, and I am not supposed to talk to strangers.

"If you missed the After-School Special, this one takes the same route. I'll even change the sign, if you'd like." He stood, reaching over his steering wheel to a small silver knob.

He turned it, and it made a whining *eek… eek…eek.* He had patches of perspiration under his arm. I do not like perspiration. I do not like noises like *eek…eek…eek.*

The words *City Center* disappeared.

That's when it all—the bus, the road, the *eeks*, the lights, Megan's questions—became too much, too big, too bright. I needed to hide, to curl myself into a corner. I wanted to bang my head and feel the rhythmic *thump…thump…thump.*

So I ran.

I ran down the slick, grassy slope beside the school. I ran across the spongy wood-chip track and through the squelching sodden grass of the school field.

I stopped only when I hit the prickly leaves of the evergreen bushes at the field's outer perimeter. Sweat soaked my T-shirt. I could smell it. Desperately I tugged off my backpack, throwing it to the ground. I yanked off my jacket. I pulled off my hoodie and flung myself onto the grass. It felt cool and wet against my skin. The air smelled of damp cedar chips mixed with moss.

I breathed, filling my belly with air. I squeezed my eyelids shut. I counted the thundering thumps of my heart. And breathed again.

***

When I opened my eyes, the sky was a black blanket patterned with stars. At first I liked lying in the darkness and counting stars, but after a while my teeth started to chatter.

I sat up and put on my hoodie and jacket. I wondered what I should do next. If I am lost, I am supposed to phone my father on my cell phone. I am only supposed to do this in an emergency, and on this occasion I wasn't really lost. I knew I was sitting at the north end of the Mount Elizabeth Middle School track.

Then I remembered that *lost* also means *unable to find one's way home*, and in this sense I was lost, because I did not know my way home. So I phoned Dad.

He came, although it was the middle of his shift. At least, he said it was the middle, but this was not strictly accurate. His day shift goes from 8:00 AM to 8:00 PM. According to my watch, it was 6:00 PM.

Therefore, he was technically five-sixths of the way through his shift.

Dad drives a 1995 blue two-door Ford Explorer with a gearshift and squeaky suspension. I heard the vehicle coming even before I saw the headlights' twin glare.

It stopped, and I opened the door and got in. The interior smelled of the aluminum smelter where Dad works, a mix of chemicals, heat, dirt and sweat.

"Here." Dad flipped open the glove box with one hand and pulled out a paper mask, the kind doctors and nurses wear. I pushed it against my face. It tickled but blocked out the other smells so that I could detect only the slight dusty smell of paper.

"I can't blow too many shifts, so for goodness' sake, don't let this happen again," Dad said, accelerating and shifting gears.

Blow means *send forth a strong current of air*.

"You understand?" he asked.

"*Blow* means *send forth a strong current of air*," I said.

Dad muttered, "It also means when I leave in the middle of my shift."

I explained that 6:00 PM wasn't the middle of his shift. Dad's cheek twitched visibly as we passed under the light of the sixth streetlamp.

"Just catch the bus," he said.

At home, Dad asked me why my jacket was wet and covered in mud. I said I'd rolled in the field.

"Why?" he asked.

I shrugged. It was too hard to explain, too hard to find the words, too hard—

I felt my body sway, rocking backward and forward.

"Jeez, it's okay. Forget I asked. I'll wash your clothes."

Dad showered downstairs, because I do not like the smelter smell of heat and chemicals. Then he made dinner. Dad says it is hard to cook for me because most foods involve smells, and I do not like smells. I cannot eat fish or onions or eggs or cauliflower or bacon. He made plain macaroni. I like plain macaroni.

After dinner I went into my room, which measures ten feet by twelve feet. I opened the music box I got for my fifth birthday. The outside is white and painted with pink and blue flowers. Inside, it is lined with pink velvet and has three tiny ballerinas.

When I wind it up, it plays "Für Elise," which was composed by Beethoven. Beethoven might have had Asperger's.

The ballerinas go around and around and around. Sometimes I count them.

After looking at them for twelve minutes, I emailed Mom on Dad's computer. (I don't have my own computer or email address.) I explained about the bus. I told her that I never knew a bus could change its name and that it had made me feel like I'd felt in Hawaii when the sea had tugged the sand from under my feet, and I'd screamed that the earth was disappearing.

Like I said, I write *a lot* better than I talk.

Mom emailed right back. She asked why I'd had a detention. I wrote back to explain that I'd missed gym because of the smells and the clanging of the metal lockers.

Mom asked a second question. She asked if Dad had told the school that I had Asperger Syndrome yet.

I wrote that I did not know.

Later Mom phoned Dad. I knew it was Mom on the phone because he called her Lisa, which is her name. Then Dad started to shout. When people shout, it means they're mad or there is an emergency or they are watching a hockey game.

There wasn't an emergency or a hockey game.

"No!" Dad's voice was so loud I could hear it through my bedroom wall. "No, Lisa! We've gone through this already. You look after your parents. Let me look after Alice for a change. And let me do it my way. Give her a chance to be a normal kid!"

I sat on my bed. Then I got out my *Webster's New World Dictionary* with the red leather cover. I looked up the definition for *normal* in my dictionary. (I had to look it up because it came after *mineralize*.)

Normal—the average in type, appearance, achievement, function and development.

I wondered why Dad wanted me to be average in type, appearance, achievement, function and development.

Average—the result obtained by adding several quantities together and then dividing this total by the number of quantities.

This didn't make sense to me. Things that don't make sense make me want to bang my head and rock.

So I opened my music box and watched my three ballerinas twirl around and around and around—like numbers that never stopped.

TWO

Lying frightens me.

I've tried to do it, but it's like looking at a tree and trying to see a house or a boat or a monkey. Besides, once I tell myself that the tree isn't a tree, the possibilities are limitless. The tree could be anything—a whale, a lion, a hot-air balloon, an army tank, a soldier with a machine gun…

I stared at page sixty-five of *The Outsiders* and wondered if I could lie about gym. Perhaps I could say I was sick, like Emma, a girl in my old school who had hated gym.

Something touched me. I jumped, jerking my gaze from page sixty-five of *The Outsiders*.

I do not like to be touched.

I turned. The guy across the aisle was leaning over, holding a piece of paper. He jerked his head toward the girl behind me like he had a neck spasm.

He was chewing gum—spearmint—and his mouth made a rhythmic squelching sound. I took the paper. It had a name scrawled on it: *TARA*.

"Alice, are you writing notes?" Ms. Burgess asked.

Ms. Burgess is the English teacher. She never allows talking on phones in her class. She walked down the row to me. She smiled. A smile can mean that a person is happy or glad or even excited. I wondered if she was happy, glad or excited.

"Answer me! Are you writing notes?" Ms. Burgess tapped her fingernail on my desk (five times). I shook my head.

"Then who is?"

"Him," I said.

The boy drew his eyebrows together and made a gesture I will not describe, as it is against the rules. He also said a swearword, which I will not write because it is also against the rules.

Ms. Burgess went red, not a solid color but mottled with white patches near her mouth and spattered across her cheeks and neck.

"I will not have that language in my class!" Her voice was high.

Then she told the boy to come with her to the principal's office. They left together. Ms. Burgess's heels *click-clacked* into the distance, followed by the heavy, slower clump of the boy's boots.

"What a rat!" The girl behind me stood, pushing her desk into mine with a clunk.

I looked at the floor. I am not afraid of rodents, as they do not bite humans unless rabid, although I don't own any myself because their cages smell.

Someone laughed. "She's, like, looking for a rat. What a moron."

Then I realized that the girl was using an idiom and meant that I was the rat. *Rat* can mean *an individual who tells someone in a position of authority about someone else's misdeeds.*

I do not like idioms.

The girl stood in front of my desk. She put both hands on it and leaned over. She smelled of hair spray and perfume.

"Do you get off on getting other people in trouble?" she asked.

"I don't know," I said.

Which was true, because I did not know what *get off* meant. My heart was pounding. I looked down at my desk and counted the lines in the grain of the fake wood.

This didn't work because the lines were wavy and merged into each other. My face felt hot and sticky. My breath came quickly, as though to keep pace with the *thump-thump-thump* of my heart. My stomach squeezed into a tight, hard ball. I felt myself start to sway, to rock.

I knew that if I rocked or banged my head, they would laugh more.

I squeezed my hands together, pressing them against my thighs. I tried to count.

"You talking to yourself? You mental or what?" the girl asked. She spoke loudly, even though she was standing close to me.

Megan said, "Leave her alone, Tara."

I hadn't even realized Megan was in the classroom.

For a second the others grew silent.

"Why? She's a nasty little snitch," Tara said.

"Just leave her alone." Megan cracked her knuckles, one at a time.

The silence seemed to grow.

"You gonna make me?" Tara asked.

"If I have to," Megan said.

I think she stood. I heard the scrape of chair legs, the jingle of her belt and the clunk of her boots. I looked up. She was coming down the aisle toward Tara, who had straightened, lifting her hands from my desk.

"Catfight!" someone yelled. (I think this is another idiom, as there were no cats about. I do not think the principal allows cats or dogs inside the school building.)

The bell rang, but no one moved.

"Well?" Megan asked.

"Whatever. I'm out of here." Tara grabbed her backpack, swinging it around so that I felt the air stir. Her runners squeaked as she walked between the desks and into the hall. The door banged shut.

People laughed. I didn't know why. People laugh at jokes or clowns or funny movies, but this wasn't any of those things.

Then everybody moved and talked at once. Feet shuffled. Books banged. Chairs scraped. I didn't move. The rule is to stay until the teacher dismisses us, and Ms. Burgess hadn't come back.

Besides, I didn't want to move. I didn't even know if I *could* move. My legs and arms felt floppy. My heart still beat too fast, and my armpits were sticky.

At last the room became silent except for slow footsteps. I looked up. Megan was walking toward me.

"She could have rearranged your face, you know," she said.

From the hall outside, I could hear the muted noise of walking and talking and the clanging of lockers. Someone had carved *JKR* into the fake wood of my desk.

"Tara could have rearranged your face," Megan repeated.

How did someone rearrange a face? I stared at the *J*. It was carved with sharp angles, no curves. I rubbed my fingers over it, feeling the roughness of the groove.

"You could say thank you," Megan said.

I said nothing.

"Or not."

The classroom door opened. I knew this without looking up because I felt a breeze and the noise from the hallway suddenly amplified.

"Hey, what are you kids still doing here? School's out." It was Principal Harris.

"Outta here," Megan said.

I looked down, watching her boots leave and counting her footsteps. Then I heard the squeak of Mr. Harris's shoes as he crossed the linoleum floor toward me. I stared at the *J*.

"You too." He'd reached my desk. He leaned forward, putting his hands over the *JKR*. He had stubby fingers with short nails and dark hairs at the knuckles. Coffee laced his breath.

"Hey? Are you okay?" His hand lifted, touching my shoulder, and then everything—the touch, the coffee breath, the squelching spearmint gum, idioms, rats, Ms. Burgess, Ms. Lawrence, Tara, Megan, Kitimat, Mom being a sandwich, buses that changed names and Dad wanting me to be average in type, appearance, achievement, function and development—became too much.

I couldn't breathe. I couldn't swallow. I couldn't even see properly. The chairs, the desks, the windows and even Mr. Harris jumped and swirled in a jerky, panicked dance.

I got up. I must have hit my thigh. I found a bruise the next morning, big and blue and purple.

Then I ran. Past the principal, the desks, through the door and into the hall.

But the hall was worse. It smelled of molten metal from industrial ed, burned food from cooking class, sweat, socks, perfume and hair spray. Lockers clanged. The intercom crackled. People laughed and shouted.

I couldn't get through. Their bodies were made huge by backpacks, and thick winter coats clogged the hallway.

Like a wall. Of bodies. Of flesh.

I couldn't stop running. I had to get out. I had to get away. I pushed through them, still running, weaving through the blur of faces, not stopping until I'd burst into the cold outside air.

And still I ran. I ran across the entry to the parking lot, down the grassy hill, across the spongy wood-chip track, stopping only at the edge of the empty field.

I doubled over, gulping. My chest hurt. My heart pounded. My eyes stung. My legs wobbled as I let my body slump until I was on my knees. The dampness of the earth soaked into the denim of my jeans.

Then I curled into a ball and squeezed my eyes tightly, tightly shut.

***

"I brought your backpack out."

I curled tighter. But I could hear noises now—the distant purr of traffic, a bird, a car door. I opened my eyes. It was dark, not pitch-black but a wintery dim.

"The bus should be here soon," Megan said, putting my pack beside me.

"The—After-School—Special?" I pulled myself into a sitting position.

"No, it's gone. You've been here for, like, an hour. But the City Center bus goes to the same place."

I swallowed. I heard the *glug* in my throat. I looked past the field to the wet road and the passing cars, their lights making streaks of brightness in the gray afternoon.

Megan sat on the grass. The chains around her neck and waist clanked.

"What do you have?" she asked.

"Have?" *Have* means *to possess or own*. "A cell phone, my agenda, my mask, one pencil, two pens, a scientific calculator, my math binder, my lunch bag, my bus pass and twenty dollars for emergencies," I said.

"No, I mean, why are you like this? Why do you act like this?"

I couldn't remember anyone ever asking me that question. Usually they asked their moms, or their moms asked my mom or the teacher.

"Asperger's," I said. "What do you have?"

"You think I have something?" Her mouth curved upward.

"You have bad hand-eye coordination," I explained.

I know the term *hand-eye coordination* from the occupational therapists' reports. I've had three since kindergarten. My hand-eye coordination is not great, but not as bad as some kids who have Asperger's.

"Hand-eye? Why do you think I have bad coordination?" she asked.

"The bruises."

She laughed. I didn't understand why, because I had not told a joke or acted like a clown. Her laughter was high. "The bruises?" she repeated.

"Do you have a designation?" Another word I've known since kindergarten, like other kids learn shapes and colors.

"Yeah—terminal idiot from a line of terminal idiots." Her laughter stopped suddenly, like it was switched off. She stared toward the road. There was a green Toyota Camry, six streetlamps, eight trees, nine houses.

Maybe she was counting them too.

It was quiet, so quiet I could hear the feathered movement of a bird flying overhead and the rustling scuffle as Megan dug the toe of her boot into the earth.

I liked that she didn't keep talking.

And that she didn't smell.

Not of sweat or perfume or shampoo.

"We should go to the bus stop," she said, breaking the hush. "You gonna be okay to take the bus?"

I didn't answer because I didn't know if I would be okay. I did not even know what *okay* meant, because it is one of those words without a clear definition—plus it comes after *mineralize*.

"I take the After-School Special every day," I said.

"The City Center bus goes to the same place as the After-School Special."

"How do you know?"

"I take it," she said. "I get detention every day."

At the far end of the road, I saw a bus turn, its headlamps twin beams of light. I heard my breath quicken. I wished there were more cars or houses or streetlamps to count.

I shook my head and hugged my knees more tightly against my chest.

Megan shifted. I heard the rustle of her clothes. "You'll miss it if you don't go now," she said.

I said nothing, pressing my face onto my knees.

"Here," she said.

I looked up. She held out her hand. A necklace of black beads lay in the center of her palm. A metallic skull hung in the middle. Perhaps she collected skulls. In Vancouver, my mother had had a friend who collected decorative mushrooms. She had mushroom plates, mushroom salt shakers and even mushroom egg cups.

"Take it," Megan said. "You can count the beads."

"I like to count," I said.

"I know. Mom too."

"Does she have Asperger's?"

"No."

I took the beads. They felt warm from her skin, smooth and polished. I curled my fingers about them. I counted them...one...two...three. There were sixty-six, which is divisible by three.

"C'mon, we can still get it. I think the driver gets a five-minute break here."

I got up, and we walked across the damp green grass of the school field toward the bus stop.

"I take the After-School Special," I said again.

"Think of City Center as another name for After-School Special."

"It has two names?"

"Kinda. Besides, if you look down, you won't be able to see the sign, you know," Megan said.

So I kept my gaze fixed on the patches of dirty snow interspersed with muddy puddles and spikes of grass. I heard the door open with a wheezing squeak of hinges.

I hesitated. It sounded the same as the After-School Special.

"It'll be okay," Megan said.

And even though I don't like the word *okay* because it doesn't have a clear definition and comes after *mineralize*, I put my foot up and stepped onto the bus.

Three

After that, I sometimes sat beside Megan when the bus was full and I couldn't sit alone. I still preferred to sit alone, but at least Megan didn't smell.

Or ask questions.

When we had detention, the bus would be empty, and we'd get off at the same stop and walk together across the City Center Mall parking lot and along Columbia Avenue until I'd turn at Kootenay Street. Megan did not turn at Kootenay Street. She lived with her mom and her stepdad in the trailer park, four streets ahead.

I didn't mind walking with Megan. I didn't know anyone else who could walk for six minutes without saying a word. Besides, I found that even if she did talk, I didn't want to thump my head or rock or curl into a corner.

I told Megan about Mom being a sandwich and looking after my grandparents.

"She'll come up here once Grandpa and Grandma are well," I said.

"You think?"

"What?" I asked.

"You think she'll come up?"

"Of course," I said.

Megan looked at me. "You have a lot to learn."

This is true. I think knowledge is infinite—that means *without end*. Therefore, everyone, even the most knowledgeable college professor, has a lot to learn.

I said this, and Megan smiled. "That wasn't quite what I meant."

Megan knew a lot about social media. I don't, although I email my mother. Megan thought I should get a data plan, so I could text.

"Why?" I asked as we waited for the bus one day after detention.

"That way you could chat with people without really talking. And it wouldn't be so confusing for you."

"Huh?"

"I mean, you like reading. What you don't like is trying to figure out if someone is mad or sad and stuff. This way they'd tell you in code."

"I like codes," I said. I'd once correctly determined my father's password on the computer using logic. It had taken me 1,003 tries.

"Texting is like code. Like, *BRB* means *be right back* and *CYA* means *see you later.*"

The bus pulled up, and we got on and sat across the aisle from each other.

"Besides, that way I could text you," Megan added.

"You'd text me?"

"Sure."

"A lot of people text," I said, thinking of all the kids I saw on the bus who held their phones like an eleventh finger or extra thumb.

"I guess."

"It is normal to text," I said.

"Sure, everyone does it."

And just then, in my stomach, right under my rib cage, I felt something like I do when I watch my ballerinas going around and around and around.

***

One afternoon Megan didn't go straight to her home in the trailer park. Instead she walked to my house and stood at the edge of the small driveway, watching me as I walked down the path and then up the three green steps to the front porch.

"Alice?" she said.

I put the key in the lock and turned it. The bolt clicked, and I pushed open my door. "Yeah?" I said, glancing back.

"Um—can I come in?" She had a black tuque pulled down low on her forehead.

"No," I said, because—well, because people do not usually come to my house, and I do not like change. It makes me want to squeeze into a corner or thump my head.

"Your dad doesn't let you have people over?"

"I don't know," I said.

I'd never asked. Actually, my mom used to invite kids over. She'd arrange playdates. I'd hated them. I'd rock and bang my head until the other kids screamed too.

I remembered with sudden clarity how Mom had cried so hard that her mascara had run in black streams down her face. *I just want to give you a normal life*, she'd said.

Again *normal—the average in type, appearance, achievement, function and development.*

"Do normal kids have playdates?" I asked Megan.

"Huh?"

"Do normal kids have playdates?" I repeated.

"What? I guess when they're, like, two." Megan turned.

I watched her walk back up the street. I watched the side-to-side swing of her backpack and listened to the *click-clack-click* of her boots.

"Megan," I said.

She didn't stop.

"Megan." I tried again, making my voice louder.

She turned.

"You can," I said.

"Huh?"

"Um—come in," I said.

Megan came back and climbed the three green steps. She stepped into our entrance, which has mud-beige carpeting and measures three feet two inches on each side. She took off her boots and walked up the three mud-beige steps and sat on the couch opposite the gas fireplace. She looked at the thirty-two-inch television, the Wii, the Xbox, the chair and the glass coffee table.

"I like your house," she said.

I thought this strange, because I do not like new places or mud-beige carpet. "Why?"

"It's quiet," she said.

"That's because the TV isn't on."

In reality, the house is not silent. I am always conscious of its sounds—the *tick-tock* of the hall clock, the quicker *tick-tick-tick* of the clock on the mantel above the gas fireplace, the intermittent hum of the refrigerator, a strange *tap-tap* in the plumbing whenever the water is running, the barking of dogs outside, the shouts from kids next door...

Megan sat on the couch, and I went to the kitchen to make a snack. After school I always have peanut butter and jelly on white bread.

"Your dad won't mind me being here?" Megan asked.

"I don't know," I said.

"Does he get mad?"

Mad is a word with multiple definitions. It can mean *angry* or *insane*. I said this to Megan.

"Does he yell?" she asked.

"Only when he watches the Canucks."

Then I turned on the television. I always watch television after school. I like to watch *Gravity Falls* and *SpongeBob*, which are animated and not shows with real live people, although real people do the voices.

I like animated shows better because it is easier to remember that they are not real.

***

Dad came home early that day because he wasn't on a full shift. He'd been called in for a few hours of overtime. Megan stood as soon as she heard the Explorer's rattle.

"I'll go." She shoved her feet into her boots, grabbed her backpack and ran down the three steps. The front door banged shut behind her.

My father entered through the basement door and came upstairs twelve minutes later, after his shower.

"Thought I heard someone leaving just when I got in," he said.

"Megan was here."

"Really?" His voice and his eyebrows went up. "Someone you met at school, eh?"

I nodded.

His mouth curved upward at the corners. "I knew it," he said. "I knew my way would work."

"You mean when you told Mom you wanted me to be average in type, appearance, achievement, function and development?"

"What?" His eyebrows drew together.

"Normal," I said.

"Um—right." He shifted his weight and started to set out the dishes for supper, even though it was not even five yet.

"She wants me to be normal too," I said.

"You've spoken to her about this?"

"No," I said. "But she said that she just wanted to give me a normal life. When I was little."

"Oh," he said.

"So you and Mom don't need to argue."

"We don't," he said. "Or not very often. Well, um, tell me about your friend."

"She's tall," I said.

Dad nodded.

"Does that mean that she is not normal?" I asked.

"No. Why?"

"Because she is not average in type, appearance, achievement, function and development."

Dad thrust his fingers through his hair, making it look rumpled and untidy. He took out two soup spoons.

"It doesn't matter if she is tall," he said after a pause.

"Even if most people are shorter."

"Yeah. Um—*normal*—just means, uh, *typical*, like the way most people behave. For instance, it is normal to like ice cream."

"I do not like licorice ice cream."

"Yeah, that's normal too. You know, everyone has favorite flavors, and some they do not like. Anyhow, did you give her a snack?"

"Who?"

"Megan."

"No," I said.

"I'll get in some chips and stuff, if you're going to be having friends over. We want to be hospitable."

Then Dad went to make dinner for us to eat at the coffee table in the living room. I heard him open a can of soup and empty its contents into the pot. He started to stir, the whisk rattling against the pot.

After we finished eating, he said he would phone Mom once we'd cleaned up. Then he started to wash the dishes, scraping the bowls and filling the sink with sudsy water that smelled of lemon. I do not mind the smell of lemon.

And as he was washing, he started to hum.

Four

On March 8, the City Center Mall parking lot disappeared.

There were no cars, no dirty mounds of snow, no empty parking spaces. Instead, every square foot was occupied. There were lights, trailers, balloons and huge machines with giant arms. The air smelled of popcorn and donuts.

I stood on the lower step of the bus and stared.

"Get off already!" somebody yelled behind me.

A kid pushed by me. He jumped onto the wet pavement. Splashes of water hit my jeans.

Other people pressed against my back. I could feel their bodies. I could smell their breath.

"Move already."

"Retard!"

"What a freak show—what's wrong with you?"

My fear grew. I was trapped between the parking lot that was not a parking lot and these angry, shouting, pushing people. My mouth felt dry.

"More like what's wrong with you?" Megan's voice bellowed from somewhere behind me in the interior of the bus. "Are you blind? The bus has two doors, you know."

"Whatever."

But I felt them move. I heard them shuffle back. I felt the space opening behind me.

"You okay?" Megan asked.

I didn't know.

"This is the fair. It comes twice a year and sets up in the parking lot," Megan said. "It doesn't look like all the rides are going yet."

"You getting off?" the bus driver shouted from his seat at the steering wheel.

"Yeah, yeah, keep your hair on," Megan said, which was strange because the bus driver was bald and did not have a lot of hair to keep on.

"You can walk home just like usual," Megan said—to me, I think.

Still I did not say anything. I did not move. The bus driver cleared his throat. "I have a schedule, you know."

"Shut up about your schedule," Megan said loudly, adding quietly to me, "Don't listen to him. Just count."

I kept the necklace she'd given me in the right pocket of my green North Face jacket. I touched it, shifting my fingers along the round, hard balls.

One...two...three...

I focused on the rubber matting that lined the step of the bus and on the dark concrete outside. At least they looked the same as usual. I shifted, moving forward, stepping out of the bus.

The door closed behind me. The bus changed gears. I heard the engine note change as it moved away.

I exhaled as I stood there, staring at the concrete, feeling the smooth beads strung along the length of the necklace.

Then I heard it. Above the bus engine's rumble, above the shouts and yells and laughter from the space that used to be the parking lot but was now filled with lights, trailers, balloons and huge machines with giant arms, I heard music.

"My music box," I said.

I took a step forward, toward the noise and the lights and the machines.

"Want to check it out?"

"*Check—a sudden stoppage of a forward course or progress*," I said. "Or *a form of payment*."

"No, I mean, do you want to go there and hear the music?"

"Um—"

"I'll go too."

"I—"

I paused, thoughts flashing through my mind. I remembered how I had taken the City Center bus with Megan, even when it was not the After-School Special.

But I remembered also that I didn't like noise and people and strange smells.

I looked up from the pavement and watched the many people walking toward the small hut with the word *Tickets* flashing in yellow neon.

"A lot of people go to the fair," I said.

"Yeah, it's, like, the thing to do in Kitimat."

"People who are average in type, appearance, achievement, function and development go to the fair?"

"What the—? Did you swallow a dictionary?"

"I like dictionaries."

"Yeah, I guess you do," Megan said.

"People who are average in type, appearance, achievement, function and development go to the fair?" I asked again.

"I guess. So, you wanna go?"

I nodded. We stepped forward. I felt a little like I did the time I'd jumped off the diving board, in that fraction of a second before I splashed into the water.

We walked past the trucks and trailers, over huge snakelike power cords and under a ride's metallic arms.

My music—"Für Elise"—came from a circular structure with flashing lights and colorful horses on silver poles. The horses were blue and pink and green, with manes of gold.

I watched as they went around and around and around, moving rhythmically up and down and up and down on their silver poles.

"My ballerinas," I said.

"It's a carousel."

"I like the carousel."

A man standing next to the carousel flipped a switch, and the horses slowed. He tightened something with a screwdriver and then started it again.

"I like the carousel," I repeated.

"You could ride, you know, when the fair opens," Megan said.

I shook my head.

"Why not?"

"Because—because—you know…"

"What?"

"Asperger's," I said.

"So? My left foot's bigger than my right. Doesn't mean I can't do stuff."

I looked at her feet. They did not look different. "They do not look different," I said.

"Jeez." Megan looked at the sky. "Wait here."

She went over to the guy. He was perched on a stool and wore a backward baseball cap. Strings of sandy hair fell into his face.

He smiled at Megan. He had bad teeth, yellow and uneven. Megan leaned into him, smiling and tossing back her long dark hair.

He looked at me, then nodded toward the carousel. "I'm giving it a final run-through anyway. I can stop it if you want to hop on."

He flipped another switch. The music stopped. The horses stopped. "Don't worry about a ticket."

"I—I—" The words had gone, disappeared.

"You can," Megan said.

"I—I—I—" My body swayed.

"You took the City Center bus," Megan said. "It was hard at first, and then you did it."

"You—"

"I'm here now. Plus, you came here to check it out."

"But—"

Megan turned to the guy. "Turn on the music again," she said.

The music started. "Für Elise." From my music box. I stepped forward, my palms slick with sweat. I took one step. And another. I lifted my leg, placing my foot on the corrugated metal of the ride's circular base. I stood on it, reaching for the gold plastic of the horse's mane.

"You okay?" the man asked.

I put my foot into the stirrup and swung my leg over so that I sat astride.

"You okay?" he asked again.

"She's good," Megan said.

And the structure started forward. The body of the horse lifted and dropped, up and down, up and down. Everything blurred as the ride gained momentum, moving forward, around and around and around.

And I was the ballerina. I was in my music box. I was…I was…

I couldn't find the words. Even in my mind, I couldn't find them.

But it didn't matter.

Five

"What the—? Get off! Do you know what time it is? I've been worried sick!"

Dad's voice woke me as if from a dream. I blinked and stared around me at a world oddly changed. The ride had stopped. The music was gone. Everything was black, punctuated only by the floodlight's harsh glare. Noises, smells, sounds swamped me—screams, laughter, the smell of hot dogs and popcorn…

Above me the huge mobile arms of other rides whirled, casting weird elongated shadows. People screamed in sync with its lifts and dives.

Dad stood on the carousel's metal platform, one hand on my horse's mane. "Whose idea was this?" he asked.

"She—I—she wouldn't get off," Megan said.

She was standing beside me, I realized.

My dad turned to her. "Who are you?"

"Megan."

"You're Megan?" His voice went up.

She nodded. "She was enjoying it. She loved it, but then she wouldn't get off."

"Did you—? You brought her here?"

Megan shrugged. "You could say."

"It's noisy and crazy. It's the worst place for her. That was a dumb idea."

"I have a lot of those." Her voice went loud. She stepped away. She was tall, almost as tall as my dad.

I saw now that there was no one else on the carousel, and that the people standing around it were silent.

"Why didn't you phone me?" he asked.

"Didn't know your number."

"If our neighbor hadn't been here and phoned me, I still wouldn't know—"

"Yeah, well, you do now." Megan turned to go.

"Look—Megan—you don't understand. You can't just dump her at a fair. She's—she's different," he said.

"Whatever. I'm outta here."

Megan tossed her hair back and stepped down from the ride. The crowd parted as she strode through it, a tall, straight, black figure.

Different—changed, altered.

I started to rock.

"Alice. Off. Now," Dad said.

I wasn't a ballerina.

I wasn't average in type, appearance, achievement, function and development.

I rocked more. I heard the low, moaning whine of my own voice. My father swore. Swearing is against the rules. I plugged my ears. I squeezed my eyes as I got off the horse, stumbling from the ride.

I fell, curling onto the hard concrete.

Someone screamed.

The noise came from my own mouth.

Dad swore again, and I stuffed my fingers deeper into my ears and curled into an even tighter ball on the cold, rough sidewalk.

***

When I opened my eyes, the crowds had moved away.

Dad was talking to a police officer. The police officer wore a uniform. I like uniforms.

"Are you okay?" the police officer asked when I sat up.

I didn't answer because I didn't know.

"This man's your dad?" He raised his voice at the end, so I knew it was a question.

I nodded.

"She got upset. She gets stressed. Doesn't do well with noise," Dad explained. His cheek twitched, a rippling movement under the grayness of stubble. "She'll be okay once she's home."

They spoke some more. Then the police officer nodded and left.

"Car," my father said. "Eyes down."

I stood. I walked. One step…two steps. I focused on the concrete, on the white lines of the empty parking stalls and the snaking power cords.

When we got into the car, my father pulled out the mask from the glove box, and I put it on. He started the engine, shifted gears and drove forward.

I looked out the car window and studied the streetlights as we drove past.

Twenty-one lights.

The indicator went *tick-tick-tick* as we turned onto Kootenay Street. Sixteen *tick-tick-ticks*. We stopped at our house. Dad switched off the engine, and it shuddered into silence. I got out, letting the mask drop from my face because the evening air was fresh. We walked up the three wooden steps.

"Bed," Dad said.

***

Later Dad came and sat beside me and made the springs whine. He pushed his hand through his hair, rumpling it into gray spikes. "Why? Why go on a carousel, like, a hundred times?" he asked.

"Thirty-nine," I said.

"Thirty-nine? *Thirty-nine*?" His voice rose in a squeak like the bedsprings. "Why?"

I did not answer because I do not like questions. Questions make me want to bang my head or curl into a corner.

He got up. I heard him sigh as he flicked off the light. "Good night," he said.

But later, as I lay in my bed, the answer to his question came.

Because...for that whole wonderful evening, I hadn't wanted to count or bang my head or squish myself into a corner.

Because...for that whole wonderful evening, I was average in type, appearance, achievement, function and development.

***

"You've never stayed out late before. Ever," Dad said over a breakfast of Cheerios and milk (I can also eat pancakes, but never eggs, because they smell bad). "You need to phone if you're going to stay out after school."

"Is that a rule?" I asked.

"Yes, yes, of course, that's a rule," he said loudly. "And that girl—is she the one who visits here after school?"

I nodded.

"She took you to the fair?"

"I got off the bus and the fair was there."

"But she said you should go?"

"She said her left foot is bigger than her right."

"She probably bullied you into it. She looks tough." Dad opened a cupboard and pulled out crispy rice cereal, which he likes better than Cheerios. "I don't know if I want you to spend time with her."

Tough—overly aggressive, brutal or rough.

"She has bruises because she has bad hand-eye coordination," I explained, because maybe Dad thought she fought a lot.

"Probably in some gang," Dad said.

Gang—a group of criminals who band together for protection and profit.

"I don't think so," I said, because Megan usually didn't spend time with other people. She walked alone to the bus and sat alone on the bus. She walked around school alone, with her music so loud I could hear it through her earbuds.

"Well, don't spend too much time with her. She's a bad influence," Dad said.

Influence—the action or process of producing effects on the actions and behavior of others.

I also wondered what *too much* meant. I prefer to know exact quantities. Like, I need eight hours of sleep. I am irritable and tired when I have less than seven.

But by the time I had formed the question, he had gone into the washroom, and I could hear the buzz of his electric razor.

***

"You should definitely get a data plan," Megan said when I saw her at the bus stop that morning.

She leaned against the bus stop, her hoodie pulled over her head.

"Why?" I asked.

"Duh. Because I was—I wanted to see how you were feeling."

"I do not have a headache, a stomach ache or a temperature," I said.

"Your dad didn't get too mad?"

I shook my head.

Across from us, the parking lot was a parking lot again. The vans, trailers and rides were gone, and the tarmac shone slickly wet.

The bus came and we got in. I sat in the corner where I could feel the vibration of the engine through my back.

I glanced at Megan. Her face looked different than it had the night before. Her left eye was swollen shut and ringed with reddish purple bruises.

I was glad that even though I have Asperger's, I do not have bad hand-eye coordination.

"What happened to your eye?" a guy on the bus asked Megan.

He stood in the aisle, holding on to the metal pole and looking down at us.

"What's it to you?" she said, her lips hardly moving.

"Got into a fight at the fair, I bet," the guy said.

Darren—I remembered his name from English class. He always sat in the back row and had a miniature skateboard that he would flip on his desktop.

"Maybe the carnies were fighting over her," a girl said, standing beside Darren and swaying as the bus started. She was also in English class. "She looks their type—rough and greasy."

"She didn't fight," I said.

"Shuddup," Megan muttered.

"How would you know?" the girl asked. Her blue eyes were outlined with thick streaks of black eyeliner.

"I was with her," I said.

"That's right. I heard you liked the carousel," Darren said and laughed, so I guessed he must have made a joke. I laughed too.

Then Darren and the girl with the black eyeliner laughed even more.

Megan did not laugh. "Shuddup!" she said really loudly. She stood, even though the bus was moving. Her hands had tightened into fists.

"Isn't that sweet—one freaky weirdo standing up for the other freaky weirdo," Darren said.

It happened fast. One second Darren stood laughing in the aisle, and the next he was lying on the floor, and everyone, even the bus driver, was screaming.

Darren swore and sat up. His nose was bloody, and I saw tears in his eyes. He rubbed his arm across his face, smearing the blood. "I'm gonna get you for this!" he said.

The girl with the black eyeliner had started to cry, and her eyeliner ran down her cheeks in inky rivers.

The bus jerked to a stop. Fortunately we were at the school. The doors swung open and the bus driver yelled, "Everyone get off!" He shouted that fighting on the bus wasn't allowed and that he would tell the principal and the police. He said that kids today were totally out of control, particularly after the fair had been to town.

But nobody got off right away except Megan.

Megan stood and walked past Darren without even looking at him. She stomped down the aisle, her boots clumping in the eerie silence.

Even though the bus was crowded, everyone made room for her. Even the bus driver stopped shouting, saying only, "I'll report this, you know."

"Whatever," she said.

And Megan strode across the field with her backpack swinging and her chains clanking.

Six

I didn't see Megan until lunch. Actually, I hadn't expected to see her because I thought she might be suspended.

But at lunch I went to my favorite stairwell—the one that used to go up to the second floor in the old wing but doesn't now that the upper floor has been closed and boarded up.

Megan was leaning against the wall, eating a slice of bread without butter or peanut butter. Her hair hung forward, half covering her face.

Megan often ate bread without anything on it. I liked this, because that way it had no smell.

"Why are you here?" she asked.

"I come here every lunch," I said.

"You do?"

I nodded. Then I sat and took out my sandwich and started to eat it. It was quiet except for the noise of chewing and the sounds from the hallway.

"You know," she said after I had finished my sandwich, "I don't know whether to be mad because you haven't even asked if I've been suspended or glad that you're not nosy like everyone else."

I didn't say anything because this was confusing. I counted the ceiling tiles.

"I am suspended, by the way."

I knew that, in school, *suspended* meant a student was not allowed to attend school because he or she was in trouble.

"For the fight?"

"Duh."

"Why did you hit Darren?"

"I was mad."

"Why?" I asked.

"Are you for real? He was calling you names."

"People often call me names," I said.

"Yeah, well, I don't let people call my friends names."

Friend—a person one knows well and is fond of.

I pictured the word in the dictionary. I saw it in tiny bold print with the letter *n*, which stands for *noun*, in brackets.

I counted ten ceiling tiles.

There are things I know are impossible for me. For example, I can't be a garbage collector.

Or a cook.

Or a lunch lady.

At my old school, Hayley MacLeod had said that I'd never have a friend.

That was two years ago on March 19.

But I do, I'd told her. *Cameron, Ellie and Shannon play with me every Wednesday at recess.*

She'd laughed. *You have a "social" group. The teacher bribes them with gold stars.*

"Do the teachers give you gold stars?" I asked Megan.

"Huh?"

"Do the teachers give you gold stars to sit with me on the bus? And now?"

"No," she said. "They'd freak if they knew I was here. I'm suspended."

"So no gold stars?"

"Like I'd do something for a gold star!"

Then I felt…I felt like I had on the carousel and like I do when I watch my ballerinas. My lips curved upward.

"I like that you don't do things for gold stars," I said.

***

Megan was on the bus later, even though she hadn't been in class. It was a different bus driver than this morning's.

The bus was crowded, so we stayed silent until we'd gotten off and were walking across the parking lot.

That's when Megan asked if she could stay overnight at my house on Friday.

I was surprised that she would want to do this. I hate staying the night in a strange place. I hate hotels. I hate strange beds. I hate the way the blankets crackle with static. I hate finding the windows in the wrong place and the lights on the clock radio red instead of green.

I asked Megan why she wanted to stay overnight.

She laughed. I wondered why, because I hadn't made a joke. "Your dad's quiet," she said.

But Dad is not quiet. He shouts, particularly when the Canucks score. And he swears when they lose, although he tries not to. Plus he likes music and has a drum from Africa made of animal skin with tufts of yak hair. Actually, this *is* quiet, because we use it as a plant stand.

"I don't think he's quiet," I said.

"You should hear my stepfather."

"Is he noisy?" I asked.

"He drinks too much."

Too much root beer makes me burp. "Does he burp?"

Megan smiled again, so I knew she was happy. "Yes," she said.

"I'll have to ask my dad," I said, because I remembered my dad had said that I shouldn't spend too much time with Megan because she was tough.

"Yeah, I don't think he likes me much," she said.

"He thinks you're tough."

Megan laughed. "That's why I like you. You don't pretend. You're honest."

This is called a compliment. My special-ed teacher told me I should return compliments.

"I like that you don't smell," I said.

***

I told Megan I'd tell her the next day if Dad said yes. Megan said again that if I had a data plan I could text.

Megan likes to text. She also likes Facebook, Twitter and Instagram. She has 201 friends on Facebook. She says it is easier to make friends on the computer. This must be true, because Megan doesn't have 201 friends at school. She doesn't talk much to people at school.

I don't have a data plan, so I said I would email. Megan looked up at the sky.

While Dad was making dinner, I asked him if kids who were average in type, appearance, achievement, function and development had sleepovers.

He stood at the stove, making chicken noodle soup. I do not mind the smell of chicken soup. He put the spoon down and then picked it up again.

"I guess," he said.

Then I asked if someone could stay overnight on Friday. Spirals of steam rose, fogging the kitchen windows. The water bubbled with a *plop... plop...plop*. The air was warm and damp.

"Megan?"

I nodded.

He threw dry Chinese noodles into the soup. They hissed and fizzled.

"You're sure she's not just using you?"

I said nothing because I didn't know what he meant by *using*, as I am not a tool like a shovel or a knife or hammer.

"I'll think about it," he said.

He continued to chop carrots with quick repetitive motions. Then he threw them into the pot so that they plopped and splashed.

"This Megan—what do you like about her?" he asked after a moment.

I tried to find the words, but too many swamped my brain. Instead I counted the tiles of the backsplash behind the sink.

There were six rows of eight.

Forty-eight.

"I like that she doesn't smell," I said at last.

My father inhaled. "She doesn't smell? A lot of girls don't smell!"

"Some use smelly shampoos and perfume."

"And Megan doesn't?"

"No."

He cut the celery and threw it in...*plop, plop, plop*...

"Why?" he muttered, grabbing another celery stick and cutting again with quick, sure strokes. "I've always wanted you to have friends and now—now you choose the local thug, and all you can say is she doesn't smell. She might murder us in our beds, but she doesn't smell."

"And," I said loudly, the words I needed to say suddenly clear in my mind, "she doesn't do things for gold stars."

***

After dinner, Dad said Megan could come over on Friday. "She can come here," he said, "but I don't want you going over there."

"I don't want to go there," I said. "I will tell her tomorrow. Although I wish I had a texting plan. Then I could text her."

Dad was washing dishes. The smell of chicken soup still lingered. "Are you getting into this high-tech stuff?"

Getting into is slang. It means *getting involved in*.

"Yes, it is easier to make friends," I said. "Megan has 201 friends."

"She would." He looked at me and pushed a damp strand of hair from his face. He opened his mouth and then closed it.

After that he turned off the tap and poured a second cup of coffee from the pot. A drop of coffee fizzled on the hot plate. He took the cup to the table and sat down heavily, so that the seat wheezed. "I guess I'd best go over the rules."

"Yes," I said. I like rules. They make me feel safe, like seat belts in cars and railings around high balconies.

"I'm not sure about Facebook, but I guess we could set you up with texting and your own email on your phone."

"And the rules?" I asked.

"Never give out your real name online. Never give out your address. Never give out your age or other identifying information."

He stirred his coffee. I watched the wisps of steam rise. I didn't know what *identifying information* meant. Dental records? That is how they identify people after a plane crash.

Or DNA and fingerprints.

I said this to Dad, and he laughed, so I guess I made another joke. He said it meant that I must not give out any information that might allow someone to find me, like my real name or my address.

"But why wouldn't I want them to find me?" I asked.

He went to the fridge for cream. "Sometimes bad people go on the Internet and pretend to be kids when they're really adults. You know, they pretend to be something they're not."

"Like my preschool teacher being a witch at Halloween?" I said.

He ran his fingers through his hair. "Not exactly. Just remember—don't give out your personal information on the Internet. It's not safe. And never agree to meet someone that you've only met online."

"Is that a rule?" I asked.

"Yes. Actually, there was a pamphlet at the library about this stuff. I thought it might be useful." He got up and started to rummage through the drawer where we keep papers like warranties and manuals. "Here."

He gave me a pamphlet with the heading *Keep your child safe online* and a picture of two kids hunched over a laptop.

"Thanks. I'll read it later," I said.

Dad nodded, sitting. "I guess it's—um—Megan who told you about this stuff?"

I nodded.

"I mean, I guess it's good. All the kids are doing it," he said.

"Good?"

"Well, um—normal."

"You mean average in type, appearance, achievement, function and development?" I asked.

Dad was silent for a second. He stirred his coffee and then laid the wet spoon on a napkin. "Yeah, I guess it is," he said.

Seven

The next time I saw Megan was at recess two days later. She was sitting at her locker. Her bruise was no longer a reddish purple but now looked a yellowish-greenish purple.

"Was it closed?" I asked, sitting beside her.

"Huh?"

"The door you walked into?" I asked, because on the bus she'd said she walked into a door.

"Sure," she said.

"But your nose isn't bruised?"

"So?"

I wondered how she could walk into a closed door without hurting her nose. But perhaps the door was open.

Or she walked into the door sideways.

"Was it a little open?" I asked.

"Huh?"

"Was the door a little open, or maybe you were on an angle or—"

"Shuddup already!" Megan spoke loudly. Her brows had drawn together like the angry face on the feelings chart my teacher at my old school gave me.

"Are you mad at me?" I asked.

"Duh!"

"Are you going to hit me?" I asked, because she had hit Darren when she was mad at him.

"No, I don't hit."

"You hit Darren."

"Jeez, let it go already."

I said nothing because I did not know what I should let go, as I was not actually holding anything. I looked at my hands, which were empty.

"Sometimes it's better not to know all the answers." She stood. Crumbs fell to the ground.

I watched as she turned and walked away, the rhinestone skull bright on her leather jacket.

I tried to count her footsteps, but they were muffled by other footsteps, the din of talking and laughter and lockers clanging.

Personally, I do not think it is ever better not to know answers. I like answers. I like to know that two plus two must equal four. Answers are like rules—the safety rails on a balcony.

I tried to think of a situation when it would be better not to know the answers, but this made me feel like I did in Hawaii when the sand had shifted under my feet. I started to rock. I counted the lockers opposite—one...two...three...

"She's talking to herself again!" a girl said.

"That is so weird." The guy next to her looked down at me, then turned away to open his locker, finding the combination with a *tick-tick-tick*. "Probably schizo."

Schizo stands for *schizophrenic.*

Schizophrenia—a mental disorder characterized by a breakdown in thought processes and often featuring auditory hallucinations and bizarre delusions.

"I am not schizophrenic," I said, standing.

"She talks!" The girl laughed.

"Well, you're weird enough. Maybe they just haven't figured it out yet," the guy said to me.

Another girl spoke up. "Hey, don't bug her." Her voice had a nasal twang. "We don't want that wacko Megan fighting us. She's butch."

"Megan is my friend," I said.

"Nothing to boast about."

"I had a cousin who was schizo," the boy added, grabbing a blue binder from his locker.

"What happened?"

"Locked her away."

"Good thing," the girl said.

"They should do that more often, my mom says. She says that crazy people turn into drug addicts and become homeless." He slammed the locker shut.

"That Megan should be locked away. She's freaky," the guy added.

Which is when I hit him.

It was not an effective hit. He did not fall to the floor or even stumble. He stepped back, putting his hand to his jaw, which had fallen open.

"What the—? What was that for?" he asked.

"I don't let people call my friends names," I said before hurrying away to the quiet of my favorite stairwell.

***

I pressed myself into the corner. I like corners.

Unfortunately, a kid sitting in a corner is noticeable.

The principal came. I didn't look up but focused instead on his brown leather shoes and his pants, which were of a thin beige fabric and should have been hemmed, because they trailed onto the floor.

"Alice? Heard there was some pushing and shoving earlier," he said.

"I did not push or shove," I explained. "I hit someone, but I do not know his name."

"This is a hands-off school," the principal said.

I nodded. (This means we are not allowed to push or hit or shove. It does not mean we have to remove our hands from our wrists.)

"We'll have to phone your dad," he said. "You'd better come to the office."

I got up, following him away from the stairs and down the linoleum hallway.

He asked me to sit in the small room beside the office. I think it was likely also a medical room. It had a bed and packages of Band-Aids. Shafts of sunlight filtered through the blinds, turning the dust motes into dancing flecks. I could hear phones and talking and occasional laughter.

Then the bell rang.

The principal had not asked me to stay for detention, so I got up because the bell means it is time to leave the school.

I went to the bus stop and took the After-School Special. Megan was not on the bus. There were no seats, so I stood, holding on to the metal pole and catching whiffs of hair spray and sweat.

***

I heard Dad's voice as soon as I came in the door. He was speaking loudly, almost yelling.

"Of course she's fine. You lot are all the same. You want cookie-cutter kids. You don't want anyone to be the slightest bit different—"

I closed the outside door and bent to take off my shoes, sitting on the first of the three steps that lead to the main floor. I figured Dad must be on the phone, because I couldn't hear any other voices.

"No, she does not need a special program," he said in the same extra-loud voice. "Don't you have more important things to do?...No, she hasn't had an assessment. She's doing great...She even has a friend. She doesn't need one of your labels."

Then he swore, and I heard the bang as he hung up the phone.

"Swearing is against the rules," I said, climbing the stairs.

"What the—? I didn't know you were home." His voice sounded like he had been running, and his face was flushed.

"I am home," I said.

"What did you hear?"

"I heard you swear, which is against the rules."

"Yeah, right—um—sorry," he said.

I nodded, because I knew that sometimes people break the rules and then they are sorry afterward.

"I am going to make a sandwich," I said.

"Right," he said.

I went into the kitchen and pulled out the loaf of bread, the jam and the peanut butter.

"Um—anything happen today?" Dad asked.

A lot of things had happened, of course. Billions of things to billions of people, so I stayed silent because I didn't know what to say.

"How were your classes?" Dad asked.

"Math and English were the same as usual. I didn't go to socials or gym."

"Any reason?"

"I hit a guy."

"So I heard. I thought we were done with hitting. Did the guy bully you or something?"

"I don't let people call my friends names," I said.

"Friends?" Dad's eyebrows pulled together. "Is this about that Megan?"

I shrugged. I do not like questions.

I took out two slices of bread, spread them with peanut butter and then reached for the jam.

Dad still stood in the kitchen. He walked to the window and then back, pushing his fingers through his hair.

"I will watch *Phineas and Ferb*."

"Right—um—good," Dad said. "Alice—"

"Yes?"

"Nothing." Dad sighed. "Look, I'm just going to the gym for a while. Maybe we can talk about this later."

It was Dad's day off. Sometimes he likes to go to the gym on his days off.

"I don't like gyms," I said. "They smell."

***

Fifty-seven minutes later I heard the knock.

At first I thought Dad had forgotten his key. I opened the door. Megan entered. This was unusual. Megan visits in the afternoon but never in the evening.

She flung down a full backpack with a heavy clunk. This was also unusual. Megan's backpack is usually empty. Megan seldom does homework.

"Would you like potato chips?" I asked.

Dad had said I should be hospitable, so now I always offered plain chips whenever Megan visited. I don't like the smell of Doritos, Cheezies, French-onion chips or nachos.

"I need a favor."

Favor—a gracious, friendly or obliging act that is freely granted.

"My father said I should offer a snack when you come over. I have plain chips. I don't like the smell of Doritos, Cheezies, French-onion chips or nachos."

"Forget the snack!" Her voice was loud.

We weren't watching a hockey game, and there wasn't an emergency.

"You have to help me." Megan shoved her hand through her black hair. She had a cut on her forehead. "If my mom's boyfriend phones, you have to say we're having a sleepover."

I took a step backward up the first of the three stairs that lead to the first floor. I did this because I am not comfortable with any change in routine. As well, Megan's boots were wet, and I could smell damp leather and foot odor.

"Tonight? But I asked Dad about Friday. Today is Wednesday."

"It doesn't matter. I'm not staying here. I'm going to Vancouver."

"Why?"

"Visiting a friend," she said.

"You have a friend in Vancouver?" I asked.

"Yeah."

"Did you live in Vancouver?" I asked.

"No."

"How did you make a friend in Vancouver if you did not live in Vancouver?"

"Online, okay? Just tell my stepdad I'm sleeping here."

"Did you give any identifying information

online?" I asked, remembering Dad's rules. I like rules. They are like the railings on a balcony.

"Huh?"

"Identifying information means your name and address, not your dental records."

"What? I—look, just say I'm here, okay?" Megan's hands balled into fists. She wore black nail polish. Her right wrist was red and swollen. "Probably no one's going to phone anyway."

"You said your stepfather might."

"Alice, please, all you have to do is say I'm here."

The smell of her boots was strong. I went up the three steps and into the kitchen. Megan followed. I opened a bag of plain chips and emptied them into a bowl. They were plain chips because I do not like the smell of Doritos, Cheezies, French-onion chips or nachos.

Or spicy sweet—another flavor.

I put the bowl on the coffee table in the living room. Megan stood in front of the mantel. She didn't sit on the couch or eat the chips.

"Alice, friends help each other." Megan reached out as if to touch me, but then she stopped. "Please, Alice, please. I don't think he'll call, but sometimes—just stall him until the bus has gone."

Stall means *a stable for an animal.* My hands got sweaty. Then I remembered that stall also means *delay.*

Or *engine failure.*

I do not like words with multiple meanings.

I started to sway.

Megan swore.

There wasn't a hockey game or an emergency.

I don't like it when people swear. It is against the rules. I don't like it when people break the rules. I don't like things that are unusual. I don't like foot odor.

I counted the tiles around the fireplace. One... two...three...

"Why would I even expect you to help? You can't even help yourself. You live in a dream world. You actually believe your mom's coming back."

Thirteen...fourteen...fifteen...

"She's not, you know. She's left you and your dad. Gone-zo."

Sixteen...seventeen...eighteen...

"She's gone. You know, not coming back."

Gone—no longer present; departed.

"My mother is in Vancouver," I said.

"And you think she's coming back? She's not. Maybe she and your dad had a fight."

"They don't fight—or not often." Then I remembered how Dad had said on the phone that he wanted Mom to look after her parents and to let him look after me. "Except they did on the phone."

"That would be it then," she said. "Adults always lie. My mom lies. Her psycho boyfriend lies."

Megan paced across the beige carpet in our living room, which measures ten feet by ten feet. Her feet made a rhythmic *pad...pad...pad.*

I did not know what *psycho boyfriend* meant. I picked up the dictionary.

"What the hell are you doing now?"

"I am looking up *psycho*," I said.

She started to laugh. People laugh when they find something funny. I was glad Megan was laughing. It was better than swearing, which is against the rules.

Then she stopped laughing and ran from the room. I heard her footsteps race down the steps and out the front door.

The door banged shut.

Eight

"Is Mom coming back?" I asked.

"What?" Dad had come home from the gym and was standing at my bedroom door.

"Is Mom coming back?" I repeated.

"Yes, of course. Grandma and Grandpa's house has sold. She just has to finish getting them packed up."

"When?"

"What?"

"When is she coming back?"

"Soon. Do you know when the game starts?"

Dad loves the Canucks.

I shrugged.

"Want dessert? I picked up ice cream on the way home," Dad said.

I shook my head even though I usually like ice cream. Dad left my room. I heard him switch on the television in the living room. I heard cheering. The hockey game must have started.

When we lived in Vancouver, Dad and Mom had gone to the Canucks games sometimes. I didn't go because I did not like the noise or the crowds or the smells from the concession.

All adults lie.

All—the whole quantity of a group.

I walked out of my room. I turned on the tap. The water splattered as I filled up my water glass. I took a drink and went into the living room.

"Yeah!" Dad shouted at the TV.

The Canucks had scored.

"Do you lie?" I asked.

"Huh?"

"Do you lie?"

"What's with all the questions tonight?"

"Megan says all adults lie."

Dad swore. "That girl has problems."

"You swore," I said.

"Yeah, yeah. I'm sorry."

"Swearing is against the rules," I said.

I stopped. I stared at the TV. I stared at Don Cherry, who wore a scarlet coat embroidered with flowers. Dad's swearing made me remember his earlier conversation, when he had used swear-words on the phone.

"You swore on the phone," I said.

"What?"

"Today," I said. I remembered his words, and I realized something else. "You lied too."

"Huh?"

"You said I didn't need a special program and that I had never had an assessment. But I have been assessed. I have had an assessment."

"Alice," Dad said. "Look. Sometimes adults—they have to tell—well—it wasn't a lie, exactly."

I turned away from the TV and Don Cherry and his scarlet coat. "Who?"

"What?"

"Who were you talking to on the phone?"

"I—"

"Because—you did. You lied."

"No," he said. "It was an omission, and I meant it for the best."

Omission comes after *mineralize.*

He pushed back his hair. "It's just—well, your mother was always telling the teachers that—well—that you are different. I just thought that a new place, fresh start...Then the file didn't arrive from the other school. And...and you were doing well...sort of. So I wanted to give you the chance of being normal."

"You lied," I repeated.

The feeling I'd had in Hawaii when the sand slipped from under my feet came again but worse—as though not only the beach but the whole world was slipping, sliding, disappearing.

"Alice—"

I walked to my room. I shut the door. I sat on my bed.

Megan was right.

Adults lied.

All adults lied.

And if he had lied about this, he might have lied about everything...anything. He might have lied a hundred, a thousand or a million times. The possibilities were endless.

My head hurt. My throat hurt. My eyes hurt. I reached for my music box. I lifted the lid and watched the ballerinas twist around and around and around.

This time it didn't help.

So I thumped my head on the floor twenty-four times.

"Alice." Dad knocked on my door.

I did not answer. I bent forward to pull out the shoe box I keep under my bed, which contains ninety-three polished rocks.

The pamphlet Dad had given me at dinner fell onto the floor. I picked it up. I read the heading *Keep your child safe online.* Underneath, I read that it's dangerous to agree to meet someone you have only met on the computer. Another heading said *Be a good friend. Help keep your friends safe.*

At least Dad had not lied about this, I thought.

I put away the pamphlet and pulled out my collection of polished rocks. I took out three and moved them between my fingers so that their polished sides clicked and clacked and clunked.

"Alice?"

Adults lie. Adults lie. Adults lie.

I heard the words with every click of the rocks.

My breath came quickly, like I'd been running in gym class. Blood *shushed* against my eardrums. I shut my eyes. I counted the rocks, pushing them through my fingers—one, two, three...

Friends help friends. Friends help friends. Friends help friends. Friends help friends.

And I—had—not—helped.

I moved the rocks faster. *Click-clack-click-clack-click-clack.* Sweat tickled my palms and dampened my armpits. My heart beat like the African dancer's drum at the last school concert.

And Mom? Dad was a liar. Dad lied. Which meant Dad might have lied about that too.

The African drum got faster and faster, wild, thundering with the words *Mom*, *friends* and *lie* crazily mixed.

I pressed my hands to my ears, stuffing my fingers in with painful force.

"Alice," Dad said.

I squeezed my eyes tightly shut, still pressing my fingers into my ears, trying to blank out the drums, Dad, everything.

"Let me in."

I threw the rocks—all ninety-three, the whole boxful—in a noisy, rattling blast against the door. They clattered to the floor.

My dad walked away. I counted his footsteps.

Then I knew what I had to do.

Nine

I got to the bus depot at 7:33 AM.

I almost didn't go. I almost stayed in my room. Then I almost stayed in our entrance hall, huddled in the corner. I almost lay down in the cool morning dampness of our yard.

But I didn't.

Instead I counted the nine rocks I had put in my pocket and walked to the bus depot.

By the time I arrived, I'd counted forty-seven cars, forty-two houses, nine fire hydrants, two stop signs and three *For Sale* signs.

My hands were sweaty, my breath came in gasps, and my heart felt as if it would beat right out of my rib cage.

The bus depot consisted of a single room with white walls, a tile floor and a counter at one end. It was quiet, empty and without any strong odors.

"You going to Vancouver?" the man behind the counter asked.

I nodded but did not speak, because he was a stranger and I am not supposed to talk to strangers.

"One way or return?"

I didn't understand. I shrugged.

"You planning on coming back here?" he asked.

I nodded.

"Then you want a return."

I bought the ticket. It cost $89, which left me with $111 from the $200 I'd brought from home. (I'd taken $200 from the $312 that I'd collected in my blue pot-bellied piggy bank with the broken ear.)

I sat on the wooden bench and counted the items in the vending machine. Skor chocolate bars (three), ketchup chips (two), salt-and-vinegar chips (three), Smarties (three), M&M's (five). Four racks were empty.

I waited. Six people came in. They didn't talk to me, which was good. One person held a coffee, clutched between his two hands as though he was cold. I don't mind the smell of coffee.

A voice crackled over the loudspeaker, even though there were only eight people in the waiting room, including the guy behind the counter. "The Prince George bus is now loading."

I stood. I needed to catch this bus, which would take me to Prince George, where I could transfer to another bus that went to Vancouver. My watch read 7:57 AM. I went outside. The bus already had its engine running. The air smelled of diesel, and I hurried to stand behind a large woman with a blue backpack that had three zippers and a koala-bear key ring dangling from its strap.

"You can get in now," the bus driver said. He wore a gray uniform.

The six other people (four women and two men) stepped onto the bus, but I waited until my watch read 8:03 AM. The bus driver went to the other side of the bus and loaded the baggage. I heard hollow thumps as he threw the bags into the vehicle's metal underbelly.

"You gonna wait all day?" the driver asked, coming back to my side.

I shook my head. *All day* is an expression. I don't like expressions. Besides, the bus driver was a stranger, and I am not supposed to talk to strangers. It is a rule. I touched the round, smooth rocks. I pushed them through my fingers—one... two...three.

Carefully I stepped onto the bus and walked into the surprising warmth of its interior. It had plush seats patterned with red and gray diamonds instead of the cracked fake leather of the school bus. It didn't smell bad, just dusty.

I sat down. I leaned my head against the window and felt the hard coldness of the glass and the vibration of the engine through my legs, arms and head. I like vibration.

The door closed. The driver sat down and shifted into gear. He swung the bus out of the lot and up the hill through Kitimat's two stoplights.

As I have said, identifying emotions is hard for me. My hands felt clammy, which indicates fear, but I felt something else as well. As we passed by the viewpoint overlooking Douglas Channel, and the Chamber of Commerce with its square of flags, and the graveyard, I felt a frothy, bubbly feeling in my stomach…

I hoped I would not get sick.

I hoped no one would get sick, because the smell of vomit makes me rock and bang my head, and this freaks people out more than vomit does.

But no one got sick. No one spoke to me, and I stared out at a landscape populated only with trees and felt the bus's engine rumble through me. We traveled along the Skeena River, and I watched its fast, turbulent movement as it twisted and turned, swollen with the runoff from the melting snow.

And then I slept.

***

The Prince George bus depot stank.

It smelled of French fries.

It smelled of onions.

It smelled of wet boots and cigarettes.

It smelled of diesel fuel and exhaust fumes.

The smells hit me the second I exited the bus. I stopped, standing quite still on the gray concrete curb. People pushed me. Someone swore.

Men laughed. A child screamed. People spoke, laughed, shouted.

"Come on, move it," someone said behind me.

I felt hands on my back.

I hate being touched.

The crowd moved forward, propelling me through two wide doors and into the terminal. This was worse. The waiting room was smaller, more crowded, and the smell of smoke, onions and French fries was stronger. Harsh fluorescent lights hurt my eyes, and sounds bounced off the low ceilings, so loud they struck me with physical force.

I saw a corner approximately ten feet away. I pushed through the crowd, holding my breath so that I would not inhale the air. At last I reached the corner. I squashed my body into its sharp angle, sliding down its length until I felt the firm, cold hardness of the linoleum floor under my butt.

I closed my eyes. I rocked so my head went *thud...thud...thud...*against the wall and my heart beat *shush...shush...shush.*

One...two...three...four...five...

I moved the rocks in my pocket with a rhythmic *click-click-click.*

Six...seven...eight...

"Miss, are you okay?"

"Hey, are you mental?"

"What a weirdo!"

"Probably drugs."

"Strung out."

"Should we, like, do something?"

"Don't stare at the lady, dear."

"Maybe we should get the police?"

"Or an ambulance."

The words and sentences invaded my space. I squeezed my eyes more tightly, shoving my fingers into my ears, pushing myself into my corner and rocking.

"Drugs for sure."

I tried to count. I couldn't. The noise, the questions, the onions, the diesel, the people—

"Alice! What—what are you doing here?"

The words came from a far distance, and it took me seconds to make sense of them. I opened my eyes—just a little, so that I could squint through my lashes.

I saw a miracle.

It was like the parting of the Red Sea. People fell silent. They backed away, stepping aside as

Megan strode forward. Her boots clunked. Her chains rattled.

"Outside," she said.

I shook my head.

"Get up."

I got up.

"Hold this." She pushed the strap of her backpack into my hand. "I'll lead the way. You close your eyes. And hold your breath."

I shut my eyes tightly. I held my breath. I gripped the strap of the backpack. She stepped forward, and I followed her into the frozen hush of the Prince George morning.

I inhaled. The air was so cold it stung my throat and lungs. When I opened my eyes, I could see the fog of my own breath.

I don't know how long we stood on the pavement. I don't remember feeling cold, although I felt Megan shivering beside me.

But after a while, I noticed my surroundings. I saw that we were standing beside a side road patterned with frost and bordered by piles of dirty snow. A row of six stores, not yet open, stood opposite. A man cleaned the windows at OK Tires. Wisps of steam rose from his bucket. Seven tires were on display.

It didn't smell.

"Why'd you come?" Megan asked.

I shrugged.

"Was it...because of what I said about your mom?" Her forehead wrinkled.

I don't like questions, particularly if I don't know the answer. Questions like *Is the earth round?* are fine because I have seen pictures taken from space in which the world looks like a green-and-blue Christmas ball.

Why did I come?

"Do your parents know anything?" Megan asked.

My parents know a lot of stuff. "My mother has a bachelor's degree in social work."

Megan breathed out. "About me...you know, being here?"

"No," I said.

I had written in the note to my dad only that I was getting the bus to Prince George.

"What about you? Did you say you were leaving?"

"No," I said.

Megan exhaled with a soft *whoosh*.

"I wrote," I said.

Megan swore. "Why?"

"It is the rule."

"The rule. Forget the rules. What did you write?"

"I wrote that I was catching the 8:00 AM bus to Prince George," I said.

"But why?"

"I am supposed to say where I am going," I said.

"No, I mean why did you follow me? If there hadn't been mechanical problems, I'd have left on an earlier bus for Vancouver. I wouldn't even be here."

My breathing got fast again because I don't like questions. I started to rock.

"Okay, okay. I'm sorry. Don't answer." Megan turned. She walked a few feet in one direction and then circled back.

We were silent. I watched the man clean the window. He lifted the squeegee five times. The intercom above us crackled. A voice piped out, loud in the still open air:

"All passengers bound for Vancouver, your bus is ready for loading."

Ten

"You should go back," Megan said.

"It is too smelly in the terminal," I said.

"No, I mean back to Kitimat."

I shook my head.

"But why?" Megan said. "Look, you can ask your mom stuff on the phone."

"Or write," I said, because I write better than I talk.

"Exactly," she said. "And they must be worried."

"Friends help friends," I said.

"What?"

"You don't do things for gold stars."

Megan pushed her hand through her hair. The silver skull ring glittered. "Gold stars?"

"You don't do things for gold stars," I repeated.

"You mean it's not about your mom. That's not why you came? You came to help me?"

I rocked. "Dad—says—you—have—a—problem."

"He would."

"Friends help friends."

"Look, I don't need—I mean, I know I asked you for a favor. I shouldn't have. But now it's fine. I'm on the bus. I'm okay. I mean, I'm well. I don't need help. Honestly, it would be better if you go back."

"Friends keep friends safe," I said.

"What?"

I pulled out the pamphlet Dad gave me. She glanced at it. Her lips twisted upward like the happy face on my feelings chart.

"You really are," she said. "Trying to look after me."

I pointed to the paper. "See? It is not safe to give out your identity on the Internet."

"Look, it's nice that you want to help. But you don't need to. I've, like, talked to Rob hundreds of times. He listens. He cares. He doesn't beat the crap out of me."

She said the last three sentences so quickly it was hard to understand. She crossed her arms. This is called body language. Or it could mean that she was mad or afraid.

Or cold.

Most likely cold, I thought.

"Final boarding announcement for all passengers bound for Vancouver," the disembodied voice announced.

Megan turned. "Stay here. There's a bus back to Kitimat later. Your dad would meet you."

I shook my head.

Megan opened her mouth like she wanted to say something and then shut it, shaking her head.

"This is a first," she finally said.

"Huh?"

Megan laughed. "No one's ever wanted to keep me safe before. And it's someone—"

Her voice trailed into silence. For a brief moment we were both quiet. Then an engine started.

"Come on," Megan said, "or we'll both miss the bus."

***

The Vancouver bus's number was 363. It was like the one from Kitimat except more crowded. I sat beside Megan, which was better than sitting beside a stranger who might smell. Plus, I am not supposed to talk to strangers.

I did not mind sitting beside Megan because she did not smell. And I could talk to her if I wanted because she was not a stranger. But usually she does not want to talk, which is also good because I do not like chitchat.

Outside, cows, horses and fields dotted the landscape. I don't mind seeing cows and horses from a car or bus window because I can't smell them. I don't like them up close because they smell.

Once, Mom and Dad took me to the petting zoo in Stanley Park in Vancouver. I screamed.

When the bus came to the Fraser River Canyon, I couldn't see cows or horses anymore. Instead, the road twisted so close to the canyon's edge that I looked straight down into the foaming, frothing white rapids. Across the canyon, a railway line threaded its way in a twisting line of silver. The road seemed carved from the mountains. In some places, wire netting hung over bare rock to protect the road from falling debris. In others, tunnels had been drilled into the mountain, gaping holes piercing the solid rock.

I counted seven.

After the canyon, we stopped at a place called Hope. This is a small community where hopeful miners stocked up before going through the Fraser Canyon to the goldfields during British Columbia's gold rush. I guess they hoped to find gold, although statistically they were more likely to die.

After Hope the highway got busier, and I closed my eyes. Everything was too much—too many lanes of traffic, too many cars, too many buildings, too many stoplights, too many people and too many buses. I counted my nine rocks and wished I was back in my room with my music box and my twirling ballerinas.

***

The Vancouver bus station was nicer than the one in Prince George. For one thing, it didn't smell. It had a high ceiling, a tile floor and a spacious, airy emptiness.

"I like this place," I said.

Megan looked at me. "It's a bus station."

We walked across the floor. It was smooth and shiny like marble.

"Do you know your mom's address?" Megan asked.

"I know my grandparents' address."

"If I get you a taxi, can you get there? Do you have enough money?"

"How much money will I need?"

Megan shrugged. "I don't know."

"I have $111.00," I said.

"That's enough."

"*Meeting an Internet acquaintance can be unsafe. It is best to avoid it entirely, but if you must meet with an Internet acquaintance, always choose a public place, and take a friend*," I recited.

"What? You've got that memorized?"

I pulled out the pamphlet. Megan took it, scanned the page, then thrust it back at me. "You can't believe everything you read. This is so dumb. It's meant for little kids. I'm tough. I can look after myself."

Dad *had* said she was tough.

I said nothing. Megan was silent. She picked at a piece of skin on her thumb with a chipped, black nail.

"Look," she said at last. "We *are* meeting in a public space—Starbucks. There'll be, like, lots of people. Now will you go to your mom's, *please*?"

"The house belongs to my grandparents, not my mother. Or it did," I said, remembering that it had been sold.

That is what my dad said.

Unless he lied.

"Well, go there. I'll phone later. Happy?"

I was not happy, because a) I have a hard time identifying feelings, so it's hard for me to know when I'm happy or when I am unhappy, and b) because I felt confused, which makes me want to bang my head. This is the opposite of happy.

"No," I said.

"Just go. I don't want to take you to meet my friend. It would look lame."

Lame means *unable to walk properly*, but it also means *poor, weak and unsatisfactory*. This is called slang. I believe Megan meant the latter definition.

"Friends need to give each other space," Megan added.

I stepped back.

"I didn't mean—" Megan began, then shrugged. "C'mon, let's go outside and get you a cab." She swung her backpack onto her back. Her heels made a clip-clopping sound as we crossed the floor.

Outside, there were colors, noises and smells. So many. Buildings, cars, streetlights, the SkyTrain, people, the McDonald's yellow arches, the Science World dome, a horn, a motorcycle's revving engine, exhaust fumes...

Too much.

I heard the pant of my breath.

It's not that I see more but that I notice more. I noticed not only the street but also the signs, the cars, the buses, the trees, the streetlights, the traffic lights, the telephone poles, the overhead wires, the three crows perched on the telephone pole. I noticed not only the bus shelter but also the toothpaste ad on its wall and the graffiti scrawled across the seven white teeth in the toothpaste ad.

And the graffiti was rude—which is against the rules and made me want to rock and bang my head.

"Look down. Count the beads," Megan said.

I rubbed my fingers along their smooth polished surfaces until we stopped at a curb.

"What's your grandparents' address?" Megan asked.

"5900 Angus Drive."

A cab was waiting, and its driver got out. He was a stranger. He wore white sneakers. I said nothing.

"Take her to 5900 Angus Drive," Megan said to him.

I rubbed the warm beads.

"Well, get in," the man said.

My heart beat really fast, and my throat felt tight. Sweat dampened my palms. I felt Megan's hand on my back.

I do not like to be touched. I moved away, sliding into the backseat. The door slammed. The car started. Something went *tick...tick...tick...*

The turn signal.

The vinyl felt sticky and sweaty under my bum. I don't like sweat.

And the air smelled musty.

The taxi swung out onto the road, and I looked down at my hands. I spread them against my thighs, pressing my fingers into the denim, watching how the cloth dimpled.

"Just down for a visit, eh?" the man asked.

I wanted to bang my head but knew I mustn't, because that freaks people out and then they look at me and touch me and hold me.

I tried to count.

I couldn't. Everything moved too fast...much too fast...buildings, balconies, windows, street signs, *yield* signs, *no parking* signs, *stop* signs, cars, buses, taxies, motorcycles, bicycles, delivery vans, trees, power poles, parking meters, streetlights, traffic lights, telephone poles, pedestrians...

Megan.

Megan stood at the crosswalk, her backpack slung over her shoulders.

That's when I broke the rules.

Eleven

I got out of the cab. It was not a want or even a need. It was a compulsion.

A compulsion is defined as *an irresistible urge to behave in a certain way, especially against one's conscious wishes.*

Without thoughts or words, I reached forward, grabbed the door handle and pulled.

The door opened, wrenching the handle out of my hand. A blast of cold air struck me, pushing me back against the seat.

The driver swore. He swerved toward the curb, jerking to a stop. I tumbled out, falling onto the concrete and scraping my hands. From behind me, I heard the driver's angry yell. For a moment, I couldn't breathe.

I stood. Traffic roared beside me. The wind tugged at my clothes, stealing my breath.

The taxi roared away.

I stood on the sidewalk.

No Megan.

With wobbling knees, I went toward a gray stone building and sat down on the sidewalk, leaning against the wall's firm, cold concrete.

I closed my eyes.

I counted the bead necklace three times. And then another three times. At last I opened my eyes. I was sitting quite close to the crosswalk. To my left, someone else sat against the wall with a cap in front of him. I wondered if he also had Asperger's and liked walls.

In Kitimat, there are only two traffic lights, but I had lived in Vancouver for thirteen years and twenty-six days, so I knew about traffic and intersections.

I do not mind traffic lights and intersections because there are rules. I like to know that when the small illuminated white man is visible I can walk, and if the red hand appears, I cannot walk.

As I looked around, I saw that there was a Starbucks on the other side of the street. I stood up. I remembered that Megan was meeting her friend there. I went to the intersection. I waited for the illuminated man. Then I stepped from the curb, counting my steps. One...two...three... When I reached the other side, I stood still, staring down at my own white-gray runners.

The door to Starbucks swung open. I smelled coffee. I like the smell of coffee. It is one of the few strong smells I like.

I inhaled.

I stepped inside, into the warmth. A girl and a woman stood behind the counter. The girl wore braces on her teeth. This reminded me of Mary-Ella at my old school. She'd worn purple elastics on her braces. This girl had plain white elastics, a yellowed, off-white color, and she had two zits on her forehead.

The woman had dark hair, glasses and a nose ring. Behind her I saw a blackboard with prices written in pink chalk. In front was a display case with baked goods: molasses cookies (two), cranberry scones (seven), low-fat crumble (six), brownies (seven).

The girl with the braces and the two zits spoke to me. "Can I help you?"

She had blond hair. An earring set with three turquoise beads dangled from her left ear.

I wanted to ask if Megan had come in, but both women were strangers. I turned away, meaning to walk out, but stopped when I saw the back of Megan's head.

Actually, this is an assumption. (An assumption is a supposition or hypothesis.) I *assumed* it was Megan because 1) the individual appeared female with long dark hair, 2) Megan had said she was coming to Starbucks and 3) a black leather jacket decorated with a rhinestone skull was slung over the chair.

The girl I thought was Megan leaned toward a man. He was facing me, so I could see him quite clearly. He wore a black T-shirt, a black leather vest and two gold chains around his neck. Sprouts of gray chest hair peeked from the neckline of the black T-shirt, and a tattoo of an anchor twisted around his left forearm.

He smiled. His teeth looked crooked and yellow.

"Megan?" I said.

The person I'd assumed was Megan looked around.

It was Megan.

"Alice? You're supposed to be in a taxi."

"I—"

I tried to find the words. I knew what I wanted to say. I could have written it. I could see the words, slippery as minnows, dancing in front of me. My heart hammered. I heard its *boom-boom-boom.*

"Count," Megan said.

I put my hand in my pocket and felt for the rocks and the smooth roundness of the bead necklace. I looked down. I tried to count the red-orange floor tiles.

"What's wrong with her?" the man asked.

"She'll be okay," Megan said.

He swore. The balloon in my lungs got bigger, pushing against my ribs like I was going to explode.

"Don't swear," Megan said. "It upsets her."

He swore again.

"I—you—" I pushed the words out.

"What a freak!" He spoke loudly. "C'mon, babe, let's get outta here."

He stood. His hand touched Megan's. He wore a gold bracelet and had a snake tattoo on his right forearm as well as the anchor on his left. Clusters of fine dark hair grew on his knuckles.

"I—don't know." Megan stood also, her face flushed.

"The city's great. You'll love it. Don't let that wack-job slow you down."

"You really think I could get a job here?" Megan asked.

I hadn't known she wanted to work at Starbucks. I couldn't work at Starbucks because then I would have to talk to strangers. Plus, even though I like the smell of coffee, I don't think I would want to smell it all the time.

"Of course," he said.

"I'd like to live in the city," Megan said.

"You're young. Ready to live life. The city's the place for you. You'll be independent. You know, live life on your own terms."

"I'd like that."

"C'mon." He stepped toward the door, reaching forward as though to take Megan's hand. "You won't regret it."

He spoke slowly, drawing out each syllable.

"No!" I said. The word came out loud.

"Look, you'll be fine. I'll get you another cab," Megan said.

"No! You—come—with," I managed.

"Not gonna happen," the man said.

I looked away and didn't say anything because he was a stranger, and I am not supposed to talk to strangers.

"Look," Megan said. "The cab'll take you to your grandparents' house. You can see your mom. Go home. I'm good. I'm going to stay here."

"At Starbucks?"

The man laughed.

"No, I mean with Rob. I'm going to live in Vancouver."

"Why?"

"He'll let me stay with him and, you know, help me get a job."

I didn't know what to say. There are some things that just *are*, like kids live in families, with a mom or a dad or a grandparent or a foster mom—even an uncle, aunt or older brother. It was like a rule, although I'd never seen it written down.

"But—he's not family."

She laughed as if I had made a joke. "I'm not that big on family."

"But—" The words had gone.

And then, even though Starbucks wasn't any noisier or smellier than before, I felt a cacophony in my head and vomit in my mouth. My hands balled into fists. My breath came in pants. Thoughts whirled. Blood thumped.

"What the—" The man moved toward me. His breath smelled of cigarettes. And coffee.

"Don't crowd her," Megan said.

"I'll do what I want." His hand was on my shoulder. I felt the hard outline of each finger. He pushed his face into mine, so close I could see red veins in his nose, so close I could see the individual hairs of his rough gray stubble, so close I could see a polka-dot pattern of pores.

Then nothing.

***

"Should I call an ambulance?"

"Maybe water?"

"What's wrong with her?"

The words came as if from a distance.

Then Megan spoke, her tone strong and clear. "Shut up and give her space."

"You're sure I shouldn't phone an ambulance?" someone asked.

"Yeah, you do that," a man's voice said. "We're outta here. Come on."

"I shouldn't leave—"

"Forget her."

My eyelids opened. From my position, curled on the cool red tile, I could see the man's cowboy boots. They were a scuffed brown, with heavy heels and pointed, turned-up toes.

"'Cause I ain't waiting," he said.

I watched the scuffed brown boots with their turned-up toes step toward the door. I watched as Megan's familiar black high-heeled boots followed. *Click-clack-click*—I counted the footsteps, pressing my body more tightly into the cold, firm wall.

"I—" Megan said.

"Your future's out there, babe." He pulled the door open, and the traffic noise suddenly became loud. "Coming?"

I heard the movement of Megan's hand as she pushed it through her hair. "I want out. I really want out. I'm sorry," Megan said.

The door closed.

***

"I'll call the ambulance," the girl with the two zits said.

"No!" I shouted. I pushed my body harder into the corner, because I do not like ambulances. I do not like sirens.

The girl stepped away. "Maybe I shouldn't? Maybe she'll get, like, violent."

The older woman came closer. I could hear the squeak of her shoes, and when I squinted I could see their white outline against the floor.

"Now, dearie," she said in a kind voice. "How about you tell us who we can call?"

"Megan," I said.

"Is that your friend, dearie? Well, I think she's made her choice. But don't you be worrying. She looks like the type that can look after herself."

I wondered what this meant. I wondered if I were the type who could look after myself. I can brush my hair. I can do laundry. I can even cook—unless I burn something. Then the smell makes me want to bang my head.

The girl with the two pimples came back with water. The older woman took it from her and put it close to me.

"Now have a drink and tell us who to call. I don't want to have to phone the police, you know."

The police?

The police wear uniforms and make people obey rules. Except I remembered that when I got lost seven years ago, the police car smelled of vomit.

Plus the police officer made me go to the police station even though I wanted to go home.

The police station had also smelled—a stuffy mix of sweat, coffee and the dusty smell of an old building.

I stood, stepping toward the exit.

"No, no. Sit down," the woman said.

She reached forward. Her hand touched my arm.

"No!"

I do not like being touched.

My heart started to *thump-thump-thump* again. Sweat prickled on my forehead.

The woman touched me again. Her hand was on my back. She smelled of perfume. I hate perfume. I hated her touch. I hated that she was going to phone the police. I hated that they might come and make me drive in a car that smelled of vomit.

"Alice."

Megan stood behind me, a few steps from the rear door. I hadn't known there was a rear door.

"You came back," I said.

"Yeah." Her lips were turning down, and her mascara had run.

"I'm—I'm glad," I said.

I sat, a hard, sudden movement as my knees buckled beneath me.

"The girl's crazy," the woman who had touched me said. "You get her under control or I'm calling the police."

"She's fine. Leave her be," Megan said. "Just stop going on about the cops."

The woman must have listened because her squeaky white shoes disappeared from my view, and Megan slid down the wall so that we were both sitting on the tile floor.

"Police?" I asked.

"No police," she said.

We sat quietly. (I do not know exactly how long because I couldn't see a clock. I like clocks.)

Also I couldn't see her friend.

"Where is he? Your friend?" I asked.

"Gone."

"Are you sad?" I asked.

Her turned-down mouth looked like the *sad* picture in the feelings chart the teacher in my old school gave me.

"Duh," she said. "Though he's a total loser."

This is slang. "Failure, dud, has-been," I said, remembering the definition in the *Webster's New World Dictionary*.

"Enough already. At least he got me outta Kitimat. Escape."

Escape means *get away, break out, get loose*. Convicts escape. Prisoners of war escape. My hamster escaped. Megan was not a hamster or a soldier or a criminal.

"Are you arrested?" I asked.

"What?"

"Is that why you need to escape? They're going to send you to jail?"

Megan's lips twisted. "I am in jail."

"You're in Starbucks."

"I've always been in jail." Megan leaned against the wall.

"They let you go to school from jail?" I asked.

"Yeah," she said. "They let me go to school."

We were silent until Megan spoke. "Anyhow, um, thanks."

"What for?"

"Being a friend. I've never had any."

This surprised me because Megan does not have Asperger's and should have typical social skills. Besides, she has 201 friends on Facebook.

We became silent again. Customers came in and out. The doorbell dinged. Both the girl with the two zits and the woman with the squeaky shoes stood behind the counter. The espresso machines fizzed and hissed. Sometimes the older woman looked at us.

"C'mon," Megan said, standing. "We'd better get you to your grandparents' before the old cow freaks again."

I got up. (*Cow* was slang for the older lady with the white, squeaky shoes.)

She leaned over the counter now and spoke to Megan. "You sure you're okay with her?"

"Yeah," Megan said.

The woman shrugged. "You know best."

Outside, traffic passed. The noise of engines was constant, like giant cats purring or hundreds of fans. I counted the floors in the building opposite.

Thirty-two—or at least thirty-two rows of windows.

Not a good number.

A cab pulled up in front of us. Its name was painted on the side: *Bluebird Taxi*. We got in. The vinyl seat creaked. Stale cigarette smoke hit me like a wall. I groaned.

"Mask," Megan said.

I pulled it out, pressing it to my face.

"To 5900 Angus," Megan said.

The mask smelled of paper. I was sweating. I could feel the stickiness in my hair and the clinging dampness of the cotton shirt against my back. The cab lurched forward. I put my free hand into my pocket and felt for the beads.

Through the window, the city flickered past—neon signs, headlights, shop windows, pedestrians huddled under umbrellas, buses, motorbikes, bicycles.

"Shut your eyes," Megan said. "Count."

I counted to 119.

"Better?" Megan asked.

I nodded. "How do you know?"

"What?"

"How—to—help?"

"My mom."

"She has Asperger's?"

"No." Megan paused, her fingers rubbing against the cloth of her jacket with a *scritch-scratch* sound. "She hallucinates."

"Schizophrenic?" I asked. Like I said, I know this language like other kids know colors and shapes.

"Addicted to meth."

"What's meth?" I asked.

"A drug."

"Does meth make her schizophrenic?"

"It makes her see spiders," Megan said.

"I don't mind bugs. They do not smell."

"She hates them."

After that we didn't speak. The taxi meter ran, the numbers clicking into place with a rhythmic, comforting *tick-tick-tick.*

Twelve

After twenty-three minutes, the cab turned down Angus Drive, maneuvering along the familiar twisting roadway under the bare branches of the maple trees. When we lived in Vancouver, we'd visited my grandparents once a week—except for last May, when Grandma broke her arm and went into the hospital, and Grandpa visited her there, so the house was empty and there was no one to visit.

The cab stopped at the curb. I opened the door and got out. The rain had stopped, but intermittent drips plopped from the trees as the wind rustled through them. One...two...three...

The air smelled of damp earth and moss. A *For Sale* sign hung to the left of the front path. A red *Sold* sticker had been pasted diagonally across it. The sign rattled in the wind.

"Money," Megan said.

"Huh?"

"Money to pay the cab."

I gave Megan my handbag, and she handed out two twenties and a ten, which equals fifty dollars. The taxi drove away.

We stared at my grandparents' house.

"A light's on," Megan said. "So someone's in."

The light shone through the diamond-paned bay windows. I took a step toward the red front steps. They'd been painted three years ago. I'd wanted to help, but the paint had smelled.

I climbed the stairs now. One...two...three... My heart hammered, and my palms felt sticky. Usually when I visit my grandparents, my palms do not feel sticky.

The front door is constructed of golden oak with a brass door knocker and a doorbell that rings the Westminster chimes. We pressed the bell, and I heard the muffled, familiar chimes.

The door opened. My grandfather stood in the doorframe. He used to be tall—six feet and three-quarters of an inch. I do not think he is that tall now, although it is hard to tell because his back is bent.

"Thank goodness," he said. "Lisa! Lisa! She's here!"

Lisa is my mother's name. It felt as though my heart had moved into my throat, which is biologically impossible, so maybe it was mucus.

My mom ran into the hall. Her hair is dark, threaded with gray. Usually it is neat, but today it looked wild, like she hadn't combed it.

"Alice, I—we—we've been so worried." Her eyes looked wet and shimmery, like she was going to cry. People cry when they are sad. I wondered if she was sad to see me. "Your father has been going out of his mind."

"You didn't lie."

"What? No. No, never." She stepped forward as though to hug me.

I moved back, bumping into Megan.

Mom stopped, and a tear rolled down her cheek. "Your dad told me you thought I wasn't coming back. That some dumb kid had told you that. But I am. Your father and I disagree sometimes, but I'm coming back. We wouldn't lie about something like that. Ever."

"Coming back?" I asked.

"Yes."

"Needed to know," I said.

It felt like I could breathe again, like some huge weight had been lifted.

Mom put out her hand so that only the tips of our fingers touched. I don't hug.

"I am so glad, so glad you're safe," she said.

"You two going to stand in the doorway all day, letting the cold air in?" Grandpa asked.

"I—no, of course not," Mom said. "And I have to phone your father. And...and who is this?"

"Megan," Megan said. "The dumb kid."

"Oh," Mom said. "I—we—come in. Look, I have to phone your dad and the police and Grandma in hospital and the neighbors, but then we can talk."

"Police? Will—come?"

"No, no, I—I don't think so. Not now that you're found," Mom said.

Mom is good at understanding, even when I can only grab one or two of those fast, slippery words.

Mom hurried into the back of the house and left Grandpa to close the oak door behind us. Looking around, I saw now that their front hall was different. The usual round rug had been picked up so that the oak floor was bare, and cardboard boxes lined the wall.

"Did you buy a lot of stuff?" I asked Grandpa.

The desk in my bedroom had come in a cardboard box, although the box wasn't as big as my desk is now. This is because the desk was flat-packed, and Dad had to assemble it. I remembered that he'd used a bad word.

"We're moving."

"To Quebec?" I asked.

"What?"

"Claire Pardieu in my class moved to Quebec," I said. We'd had a cake with cream-cheese icing.

"We're going to a home," Grandpa said. He spoke loudly, and his eyebrows pulled together. "Actually, your grandma's already there."

"You already have a home," I said.

"That's what I've been saying." He turned and, leaning on his walker, shuffled past the boxes and down the hall.

We followed him into the kitchen. It also looked different. Grandpa's clock had been taken down, and all that remained was the wallpaper with its familiar pattern of teapots and roses. I missed its steady, rhythmic tick. The spice rack had gone, as had the copper saucepans that used to hang from the ceiling. Everything—the ladles, the Henckel knives, the cookbooks and Grandma's collection of silver teaspoons, which I'd always counted—gone.

I'd often counted the roses on the wallpaper too—thirty-six.

Mom came into the kitchen. "Your dad is very relieved you're safe, and—uh—Megan—uh—thank you for getting her here."

Mom spoke slowly and quietly, like she was being careful. Megan did not talk slowly or quietly.

"What a line of crap. You sound like a social worker."

"She used to be a social worker," I said.

"Should have known," Megan said. She folded her arms across her chest, the chains at her waist jangling.

Mom flushed. "Look, Megan, I know you and my husband had words. And you said some stuff you shouldn't, but the truth is that Alice would never have made it here safely without you. Vancouver can be dangerous for a girl on her own. And Alice—well—for her it would be worse."

"Yeah? And that's the dumbest thing you've said yet. Alice made it to Prince George just fine on her own," Megan said.

Mom's forehead crinkled. "But—I thought she left and you followed."

"Other way 'round."

"Oh." Mom's forehead puckered again. "Well, tell me everything later. Do you want something to eat or drink? I have orange juice."

Mom gives me orange juice because I cannot drink milk.

"Yes," I said, because I realized I was thirsty and hungry.

"Whatever," Megan said. "I'm not staying long."

Mom poured a glass for each of us. Then she stopped, her hand jerking so that the juice splashed onto the counter. "Oh. I phoned your dad and the police, but I must let the neighbors up the street know. I asked them to look out for you," she said, speaking in hurried staccato sentences.

Even though she was wearing slippers, her footsteps sounded loud to me against the bare hardwood floor. Grandma and Grandpa had had a runner before, made in Persia. Persia is not called Persia anymore.

"Alice." Megan circled her finger around the rim of her glass so that it made a high, thin whine. "I won't stay."

I wondered where she would go if she didn't stay. But I couldn't find the words. She looked down at her glass as though studying her finger as it circled the rim.

I did not like the high whine. I pressed my fingers to my ears, and Megan's finger stopped. "Sorry," she said.

"If you are not staying here, are you going back to Kitimat?" I asked at last.

She shrugged. "Dunno."

"Oh." I stared at the wallpaper. I could hear Mom on the phone, her voice echoing in the empty hallway. The hallway measures four feet by twelve feet.

"Why do you care?" Megan asked. "Why do you even want to be my friend?"

"Gold stars."

"Huh?"

"You don't do things for gold stars," I said.

"Yeah, well, it would probably be better if you hung around people who do. They'd listen to the teacher. They wouldn't have told you your mom wasn't coming back. They wouldn't be so stupid."

I studied the thirty-six roses on the wallpaper. "And you don't smell."

Megan laughed. "I don't smell?"

"I liked sitting on the bus with you because you don't smell."

"You're my only friend, and you like me because I don't smell. What does that say about me?" She started to laugh and then to cry.

Laughing means you are happy. Crying means you are sad. This made my head hurt.

And I also had a peculiar, squeezing, aching feeling in my chest that I hadn't felt before.

Megan turned. She picked up her backpack, swinging it onto her back. "See ya."

"But where are you going?"

"Just leave it."

That is another phrase I don't like. *It* is a pronoun, which stands in place of a noun, but I didn't know what the noun was and I didn't know what I was supposed to leave.

"Where—what—?" I managed.

She stared at me, her eyes shiny and her face pink. "Not home, that's for sure. You can tell my stepfather that from me. I'm not coming home."

But I didn't know her stepfather. I had never met him, and I am not supposed to talk to strangers. "Can—I—write it?" I asked, because I can write to a stranger if I don't give him my address.

Megan pushed her hand through the dark tangles of her hair and laughed again. "You know—you know why I like you? You don't lie. You don't promise stuff you can't deliver. You don't say everything will be all right when it won't. You don't say you'll do something when you won't. Or you'll leave him when you won't. Or—or crap like that."

Crap is a bad word. And I didn't understand a lot of what Megan had said, so I pressed my hands to my ears.

Mom came back. Megan straightened, so that she seemed even taller in the small kitchen. I saw Mom step forward, but Megan backed away, her glance darting about the bare kitchen.

"You can't go," Mom said so loudly that I could hear her even through my hands. "I need to phone someone—your family must be worried." Mom put her hand out, touching the black leather of Megan's sleeve.

But Megan swung around. Her backpack hit the counter with a thwack. "Don't touch me." Her hands balled into fists as she jerked her body backward.

"I can help—"

"No adult ever helped me."

"I—I can try," Mom said.

"I don't need your help. I don't need anyone. Just leave me alone."

Then Megan pushed past Mom and left. I heard her boots clumping down the bare hall. I heard the front door open and slam. The noise was huge in the empty house.

Thirteen

I picked up my rain jacket and walked past Mom.

"Alice, what—where are you going?" Mom asked. Her voice squeaked.

"Megan," I said.

"Alice, sit down! Now!"

"Friends help friends," I said.

"Megan looks capable. You know, like she can look after herself. She's tough. There's nothing you can do."

"You said Vancouver was dangerous for a girl on her own."

"I can call the police. They can do something. You can't."

"Friends help friends."

"You can't just go out alone," she said.

"I will not be alone after I find Megan."

"Do you know how worried we've been?"

I shook my head, because it is hard for anyone to know another person's experience. Then I realized that Grandpa had entered the kitchen and was standing in the doorway, stooping low over his walker.

"Let her go," he said.

Mom swung around. "What! Are you crazy? I'm not going to let her walk out and tramp around Vancouver alone."

"We're on Angus Drive. Not East Hastings. She's been walking about this neighborhood most of her life."

"But—"

"She's safer than most kids. You know she'll not talk to strangers."

"I will not talk to strangers," I said. "It is a rule."

Grandpa looked at Mom, and his eyebrows lifted. She opened her mouth, and her eyebrows pulled together. “But what if there’s smelly garbage or too much noise or, well, you know, any number of things? I mean, someone needs to look after her.”

Grandpa shrugged. “Maybe it’s Alice’s turn to look after someone.”

“But she can’t—”

Mom looked at him and at me. She bit her lip.

“It’s a good feeling to help someone,” he said.

“Yes, but—I mean, that girl, Megan, looks troubled. She needs—well—she needs a lot more than Alice can give her.”

“Maybe. But what she needs and what she’ll accept—well, that’s another matter,” Grandpa said.

I saw Mom’s gaze shift between us.

“It’s a good feeling to help someone, to be needed,” he said again.

There was a silence. Not even broken by the ticking of a clock, because it had gone, leaving only its yellowed outline on the teapot-and-rose wallpaper.

I put on my raincoat.

At last Mom shrugged. “But be back in an hour and...and don’t leave the neighborhood. Keep to 41st. And don’t—don’t get on any buses alone.”

***

I walked toward the nearest bus stop, which is at Granville and 41st. Grandma and I had sometimes met Grandpa there after the doctor had taken away his driver's license.

I counted my steps.

I was at sixty-seven when I saw Megan, a tall black silhouette outlined against green grass and shrubs.

She must have heard my approach. She turned. "Alice? Can't you just leave me alone?"

"Where are you going?" I asked.

She shrugged.

"Kitimat?"

"No!" The word blasted from her.

"Then is this—are you—running away?" I asked.

"What?"

"Are—you—running—away—from—home?" I said again.

"I—yeah, I guess."

"*Most adolescents who run away return home after two days, but those who do not return often become involved in stealing, begging, prostitution and Dumpster diving,*" I said.

I do not know what Dumpster diving is. I do not even like real-life diving in a swimming pool, because I do not like the smell of chlorine or getting water up my nose.

"What the—? Jeez, did you swallow an encyclopedia?"

"No," I said.

It would be hard to swallow an encyclopedia because encyclopedias are big books.

Actually, I had read an article about adolescent runaways in *Maclean's* magazine. Dad had brought it home and put it in the bathroom. Dad likes to read in the bathroom.

"Look, Alice, I know you mean well, but leave me alone. If you want to be my friend, leave me alone! Give me space!"

Megan shouted the last words and turned, walking up the hill toward the whooshing rush of traffic.

Space—unlimited room or expanse extending in all directions and in which all things can exist.

The definition circled my mind. I'd looked it up for a science project, which was why I knew the definition even though *space* comes after *mineralize.*

I heard a bus approach. The buses in Vancouver run on trolley lines. Poles are attached to the buses' roofs and connect to overhead wires strung above the roads. Trolley buses do not smell of diesel or gas. They run on electricity and make a low rumble and a *click-click-click* as the poles move on the twin overhead wires.

Mom had said not to get on the bus.

"Don't get on the bus," I said as Megan moved toward the bus stop.

"I *am* getting on the bus."

"But—" Mom had said not to get on the bus *alone.* "I'll come too then," I said.

The bus stopped with a squeak of its brakes, and the door swung open. The driver looked out.

Megan turned to me. "Stay! I don't want you to come!"

"But Mom said not to get on the bus alone."

Megan swore. "She meant for you, not me." She stepped forward, placing one foot on the step.

Swearing is against the rules. Friends help friends.

I looked down, running the beads through my fingers.

Megan swore again. "Just leave me alone!"

I started to rock.

"Okay, okay. Enough already." Megan turned, almost stumbling into me.

"You kids coming?" the bus driver shouted.

"No!" Megan yelled, stepping back.

"Suit yourself." The doors closed. The bus moved away.

We stood facing each other. Megan put her hands at her hips, her fingers curved into fists. "A month ago you couldn't even get on a bus in Kitimat if it didn't say *After-School Special*, and now you're, like, ready to follow me on a bus across Vancouver?"

She must have been angry, because she was shouting and there wasn't a sports game or an emergency. Plus her face was red.

I looked down at my runners. "You must not go," I said.

"I can do what I want."

"Mom said it wasn't safe for you to go alone."

"Your mom—" Megan didn't finish the sentence.

"My mom doesn't lie," I said.

Megan's fists tightened. "Great—your mom's a freak of nature. She's an adult who doesn't lie, probably the only one on the whole planet. Sure doesn't help me much."

I sat on the sidewalk. I looked at my runners. I felt my rocks, running them through my fingers.

"Just let me get on the next bus," she said. "Then you can go back to your mom and play happy family."

One...two...three...four...

"You'll be better off without me anyhow," she said. "I don't know why you give a crap."

"No gold stars," I said.

"Yeah, yeah, I know. You said. Plus I don't smell. But there are other people who don't smell and don't do things for gold stars."

"Who?"

"I don't know." She threw herself on the grass beside the sidewalk and stared at the sky. "People."

We didn't speak. Finally Megan sat up and picked at the grass. She sprinkled it like green confetti over her boots.

"You've got to understand. I don't want to go back," she said.

"Because of the bus trip?"

"No. Because I don't want to live with my mom and stepdad," she said.

I wondered why, but I didn't ask because I don't like it when people ask me questions.

"I—" She pulled at the grass, yanking out clumps, the dirt still clinging to the roots. "He's a jerk."

Jerk—a quick, sharp, sudden movement.

"He's mean," she said.

I still didn't understand.

"Do I have to spell it out? He hits me." She threw a handful of torn grass.

Hit—to bring one's hand or a tool or a weapon into contact with someone or something quickly and forcefully.

"But that is wrong," I said.

Megan laughed. "Duh."

"That is hands-on behavior."

"Yeah, well, guess what. He missed that lecture." She laughed again.

"You should tell an adult, or call the police."

I remembered a police officer, Constable McNaughty, who had visited our old school. He'd said that if someone was hurting us, we should tell an adult.

"I can phone Constable McNaughty," I said.

"No!" Megan shouted the word, twisting her body so that she faced me. "No! Don't! Don't interfere. You've done enough. And it will make things worse. I only told you so you'd understand why I can't go back and...and so you'd stop following me around Vancouver."

"But he did something wrong. He should be punished."

Megan shrugged. "I wish I lived in your world."

"But you do."

"Nah, not so much."

I wondered what she meant. Only a few people, like astronauts, had been out of our world. "You are not an astronaut," I said.

"No, no. It's not that. I mean, everything is so black and white in your world."

This is also not true. Asperger's does not result in color blindness. "I perceive colors like anyone else," I said.

"I didn't mean...whatever."

Then I remembered how Dad had said that she looked like a girl with a problem. "So that is your problem. Your stepfather hitting you. That is a problem."

"Yeah, you could say."

"So you don't actually have bad hand-eye coordination. Those bruises?"

"Him. So you understand now. And you'll let me get on the bus?"

"It is against the rules to hit. You should tell the police," I repeated.

Megan stood. The chains on her belt rattled. I stood also. She pushed her fingers through her hair. "Do you know what they'd do if I told your Constable McNaughty?"

I shook my head.

"They'd put me in foster care."

"Is that bad?" I asked.

"Don't you know anything? Yeah, it's bad. Besides, my stepdad would find a way to get back at me or take it out on my mom."

Again I was silent. I wasn't sure what *take it out* meant.

"Alice," Megan said after a moment, her voice so soft I had to lean forward to hear her. "I can't go back. I'm scared."

"Count. I count when I am scared," I said.

"Then I'd be counting forever...to...like, infinity. Some things, you know, like a bus ride—they end. This—this doesn't end. It—it gets worse."

"My mom says running away doesn't fix a problem."

"That's dumb, and you know what? Your mom's dumb sayings and all your dumb rules—they don't work in the real world."

I didn't know what to say. I felt like I had in Hawaii, the sand disappearing under my feet.

I remembered that when I was in kindergarten a boy had hit me with a Thomas train. The teacher had taken the Thomas train away because hitting was against the rules. Then he had hit me with a plastic dinosaur. And the teacher had taken the dinosaur away because hitting was against the rules.

"Hitting is against the rules," I said.

"And that's all that matters?"

"Yes," I said.

***

"Come on," Megan said, standing up with a rattle of chains.

We'd sat on the grass so long that my legs were numb and the rear of my pants felt damp.

"Where?"

"Your house, I guess," Megan said.

"It is my grandparents' house, and it is sold. You're not running away?"

She shook her head. "Not today."

We stood and slowly walked back down the hill toward my grandparents' house. I counted our footsteps. When we went in, I saw Mom standing at the stove. Steam rose from a saucepan and something boiled with a *plop-plop-plop*.

"Thank goodness," she said when we walked in.

"Told you she could look after herself," Grandpa said. He stood in the place where the kitchen table had been, leaning on his walker.

"I got a saucepan and a couple of bowls out of the packing box if you want soup," Mom said.

"Four bowls," I said.

The kitchen smelled of chicken soup. This is a good smell.

"Nah, I don't need food," Megan said.

Mom said nothing but ladled the soup into the bowls, putting one in front of Megan. The table was gone, so we sat on stools at the counter.

"I'm glad you came back," Mom said to Megan.

Megan shrugged with a jangle of chains. "Why would you care?" She traced her finger along the metal outline of the spoon, not picking it up. Spirals of steam rose from her bowl.

"Because..." Mom paused. "Because Alice wouldn't have come home without you."

The corners of Megan's mouth lifted. "I guess that's true."

***

The moving van came the next day. Megan and I had slept in sleeping bags that Mom had also pulled out of a box. I slept in the room upstairs. I'd slept there before, so at least the window was in the right place.

In the morning, we'd rolled up the sleeping bags and stuffed them back into the box. We'd also cleaned the bowls and the saucepan and packed them as well.

Mom had said that I could stay with her at a hotel for a few days, just until we got my grand-parents unpacked and settled, and then we could go home. She said Megan could stay too.

I do not like staying in hotels, but I didn't want to go on the bus again. Besides, Mom said that she would get a suite, even though it was expensive, so I could have my own room, and that she would make sure that it was nonsmoking and was not near the kitchen or the swimming pool.

Megan didn't say anything. She didn't say she would stay with us, but she didn't say she would not. I didn't ask because I do not like being asked questions.

Most of the morning, Megan and I stood silently at the front window, staring at the maple trees and watching the moving men load Grandma and Grandpa's belongings into the van. A lot of pieces were going to storage because there was no room for them at the old-age home.

The spring sunshine shone through the diamond-paned frames. It felt almost warm, and I didn't mind standing there and counting the boxes as they were piled into the van.

At last Megan spoke. "I think you're brave, you know."

I blinked. *Brave* means *willing to face danger, pain or trouble; not afraid; having courage.*

"I screamed every morning in kindergarten," I said.

"People think I'm tough. I'm not."

"But..." I thought about how tall she was and how the kids stepped to one side when she walked by and how she had helped me take the bus and go on the carousel.

"You're braver than me. You're the bravest person I know. You're like a hero." Megan spoke the words in a rush.

Hero comes before *mineralize.* It means *a person admired for his or her great deeds.*

"I haven't done any great deeds," I said.

"Your whole life is a great deed. You're always doing things even when you're freaked."

"Counting helps," I said.

Megan smiled. She put out her hand, spreading her fingers so that our fingertips touched. "I've decided to be like you," she said.

"You can't catch Asperger's." There are some things, like colds and flu and chicken pox, that people can catch through viruses. Asperger's isn't one of them.

"I mean, I'm going to do things even when I'm scared."

"What are you going to do?"

"I'm going to tell a social worker about my stepdad."

She spoke loudly, her words reverberating around the empty house like she was making a presentation in front of the class or onstage.

"My mom is a social worker," I said. "Maybe you could talk to her. But what are you going to tell?" I asked.

"That my stepfather hits me and my mom."

"Hitting is against the rules," I said.

"Yes." Megan started to laugh "It really is that simple, isn't it?"

She put her hand up, and our fingertips touched again.

"A hero?" I said in wonder. I had not thought I could be a hero.

Just like I had not thought I could be a friend.

I smiled, aware of a tingling, bubbling feeling in my body. I remembered going around and around on the carousel and how my chest had felt warm and full and fluttery.

"But are heroes average in type, appearance, achievement, function and development?" I asked.

"Huh?"

"Is a hero average in type, appearance, achievement, function and development?" I repeated.

"Heroes are not average. That's what makes them special." Megan looked at me. "You okay?"

"Yes," I said, even though I usually do not like questions. "Yes, definitely. I am...okay."

Epilogue

My mother stopped being a sandwich and we flew home—Mom and Megan and I. (Mom flew back down to Vancouver two weeks later to make certain that Grandpa and Grandma were still doing fine and adjusting to their new home. Then she came back and stayed with us in Kitimat.)

Megan told the Ministry for Children and Family Development that her stepdad hit her. She did not go into foster care because Mom arranged for her to stay with us. Mom is a social worker, although she doesn't have a job right now.

Mom and Dad argued about telling the school that I have Asperger's. Mom said that it would be better if the teachers knew. She said that she'd contact my old school and find out what had happened to the confidential file. Then it would be sent to my new school.

She said that once the teachers and the principal knew I had Asperger's, they would make *accommodations* and I wouldn't get detentions.

Accommodations doesn't have anything to do with hotels. It means that the teachers would understand me better and I wouldn't have to change for gym in the locker room or go to cooking class if the recipe included onions.

Dad said that detentions hadn't done me any harm. They'd done me good, if anything. It was good luck that the file had never arrived, and we shouldn't interfere now.

That's when I told them to stop arguing.

I said, "I will decide. If I can be a hero, I can decide what we should tell my teachers."

After that, Mom and Dad looked at each other.

"You know, I think you're right," Dad said.

"But—" Mom started, a frown puckering her forehead.

"I am a hero *and* a friend," I said. "Besides, this is about me. So I should decide."

Mom lips curved upward. "I think you're growing up," she said.

"I am five feet five inches."

Mom's lips curved upward more. "Fine. It is your decision. You decide."

I went to my room. I opened my music box. I wound it up and watched the ballerinas twirl and twirl and twirl.

I watched for forty-five minutes, and then I made my decision. I decided that I would tell my principal and my teachers that I have Asperger Syndrome. We would phone my old school and find the confidential file. Then my teachers would understand me better and not get angry when I couldn't go to cooking class or change in the locker room.

Yes, I would tell them that I have Asperger's.

But I would also tell them that I was a friend and I was a hero.

I would tell them that I was not average in type, appearance, achievement, function and development.

But then, being average is highly overrated.

And, average or not, I was okay.

Totally, completely and absolutely okay.

Acknowledgments

I acknowledge the love, support, patience and encouragement of my family, who have put up with my continued fascination with the written word and long hours tapping at the keyboard. And, as always, I will be forever grateful to my mother and father, who taught me to love reading and books.

Author's note

This is a work of fiction. Names, characters, businesses, places, events and incidents are either the products of the author's imagination or used in a fictitious manner. Any resemblance to actual persons, living or dead, or actual events is purely coincidental.

Kathleen Cherry lives in northern British Columbia with her husband and two daughters. She is a school counselor and is currently pursuing her doctoral degree in psychology. Kathleen loves working with children and empowering them to develop their creativity through writing. She enjoys visiting school classrooms and libraries. As well as writing, Kathleen also loves to run, travel and read. For more information, visit www.kathleencherry.ca.